FACE-OFF

"You got a smart mouth, McCoy," the sheriff said. "One of these days I'll shut it for you, permanently."

"Is that a threat, Sheriff? I understand you and your deputies shot down eleven men and one woman in the past four months."

"Line of duty. They were all low-class riffraff."

"Like the preacher, Fowler? That kind of riffraff?"

The sheriff quivered with rage. His eyes bulged, his hands hovered over his gun butts again.

"What's the matter, Sheriff? Isn't Pistol Pete here to back up your hand anymore?"

The sheriff roared in fury and charged McCoy. The big man waited until the last second, spun aside and slammed his fist down on the sheriff's neck as he careened past. Sheriff Johnson kept right on going, rammed into a bar chair, tipped over a table and rolled on his back.

"Johnson, you're all through in this town," Spur said. "Pull off that badge right now and ride just as far and as fast as you can before the good people of this town rise up and shoot you so full of holes they'll use you for a drain gauge."

Also in the Spur Series:

SPUR #5

WYOMING WENCH

DIRK FLETCHER

LEISURE BOOKS NEW YORK CITY

A LEISURE BOOK®

October 2003

Published by

Dorchester Publishing Co., Inc.
200 Madison Avenue
New York, NY 10016

ISBN 0-8439-2135-8

The name "Leisure Books" and the stylized "L" with design are trademarks of Dorchester Publishing Co., Inc.

Printed in the United States of America.

Visit us on the web at www.dorchesterpub.com.

WYOMING
WENCH

CHAPTER ONE

May 14, 1872

(Yellowstone National Park was set aside as a national preserve by Congress in 1872. U. S. Grant was President and Hamilton Fish of New York was his Secretary of State. The adding machine which could print totals and subtotals was patented by E. D. Barbour in Boston. The U.S. census for 1870 showed 38,558,371 people in the nation. This was a seven million increase over 1860 or almost 18%. James Fisk and Jay Gould's corrupt Erie Ring collapsed. The United States Congress abolished the federal income tax. The Post Office Department became an executive

department of government. Popular Science Monthly *was published for the first time. The first Catholic Presidential candidate, Charles O'Connor, was nominated. Susan B. Anthony was arrested for attempting to vote in New York. On November 6, 1872 President Grant was re-elected.)*

Spur McCoy was not putting up much of a fight. He gave a pair of half-hearted swings, then let a telegraph round house right clip his jaw and spin him around. He should get a medal for acting, he thought, as he fell into the dust of an alley next to the stagecoach station in the northern Wyoming crossroads cowtown called Elk Creek.

"Stay down, asshole!" the big man over Spur roared. "I'm bruising my knuckles and you're not worth it." The man talking was Tyler Johnson, Sheriff of River Bend County. Johnson stood over McCoy, fists still clenched.

"I run this county, asshole! I don't like your looks and want you out of here on the next stage. Problem is, it don't come for a week. So you peddle your knives and keep your big nose out of county business. Otherwise I'll drag you out of town behind my horse until you're skinned alive." He kicked Spur in the side. "You get the message?"

Spur looked up, he was shaking, his head bobbing. "Yes, sir. I am certain that I understand your directions. I will do my utmost, Mr. Sheriff, to handle myself with the required decorum."

8

"Christ, an *over-educated* asshole! I don't even know what he's saying." Sheriff Johnson took one long look at him, went back to the open knife sample case in the dirt and picked out a six-inch sheath knife. "I'll take this here blade as a gift from you, drummer. Any complaints?"

"Absolutely none, sir. It is my privilege to serve you and to be in your remarkable little town."

"Yeah, right. One week. Remember that." The sheriff turned and walked into the darkening street. Lights came on in buildings. Spur sat up in the dust. He had rolled with most of the punches, but one had taken a gash out of his cheek. He'd get that looked at as soon as he got a hotel room.

He started to rise when a door opened in the building behind him and two women rushed out. One knelt in the dust beside him and touched a handkerchief to his cheek.

"You're hurt. We'll help you. Come inside here and I'll fix up that cheek in no time, give you a drink and get you cleaned up."

Spur took his hat which the other woman had picked up. The beat-up hat didn't match his black suit. It was a low-crowned light brown, with a wide brim and a row of Mexican silver centavos pieces around the band.

"Not necessary, ma'am. I'm not hurt."

"You *are* hurt, and bleeding. Not a gracious way to greet a stranger. Our sheriff is crude and overbearing. I won't take no for an answer."

Spur looked closer at her through the shadows. She wore a calico print dress buttoned tight to

9

her chin. Shoulder length blonde hair had been curled and framed a round face with high cheekbones and greenish eyes. He couldn't see much else before the women took his arms and walked him into the building. The smaller woman went back for his sample case and lugged it into the room, then brought in his carpetbag. The girl with green eyes turned up the lamp on a dresser. He saw at once that it was a bedroom, perhaps in one of the two hotels in town—he wasn't sure. The other girl was gone, the door closed.

In the light he saw the concern on the blonde woman's face as she washed his cheek and applied some ointment to the cut. It stung.

She sat beside him on the bed and began opening the buttons on the top of her dress.

"I'm terribly sorry the sheriff gave you such an unpleasant impression of our town. It really isn't that bad. We have some fine people here and they are interested in seeing that you stay around, and that you are treated right."

Spur looked at her, fascinated. The buttons were coming open, one by one, proving that she was a full-busted woman on the plump side. She smiled.

"Heard you tell the sheriff your name was Spur McCoy. That's a good name. Spur, this dress is just so tight I have to loosen it. I hope you don't mind."

"Don't mind at all, ma'am."

"Good," she said and leaned in and kissed his lips full and hard. Her tongue brushed at them until he opened them for her. Her tongue darted

10

into his mouth and she gave a little sigh as her arms came around him.

She didn't let the kiss end as she pulled him down on top of her on the big bed. Her legs spread apart so he lay fully on her and could feel the heat of her body through the clothes. One of her hands worked between them and massaged the growing bulge at his crotch. Her other arm crooked around his neck, pinning his mouth to hers.

She moaned softly with anticipation and let go of his neck. He leaned up and looked at her smiling face.

"Oh yes! You feel so good lying on me this way. I can feel your big thing down there pushing against me! My name is Jodi, and I don't never like to see a big hunk of new man like you come to town and get run plumb out before I get a chance or two at him." She frowned. "Oh, lordy, I hope you don't mind!"

Spur kissed her soft lips twice, then quickly twice more and her nose once.

"Why the fuck should I mind, Jodi?"

"Great! If there is one thing I really love it is a quick one that you don't expect. You know what I mean? Just bumping into somebody, and liking him and trying to get my dress open and letting him look at my titties quick."

Spur helped her, undoing the rest of the buttons to her waist, then lifting the lacy chemise.

"My god! At last I've found the Rocky Mountains!"

She laughed. "You are so nice! But wait until I

sit up and let them hang down to you."

Spur had to use one hand to hold himself up. With the other he caressed her big breasts. The areolas were large and dark brownish red, and her nipples by now were extended and bloated with hot blood. He bent and kissed one and felt her hips pumping hard at him.

"Oh, damn!" She wailed. "I'm climaxing already! Oh, god. Oh, shit but that is good! Great. Great. Great!" Her voice rose in a wailing tribute to kisses and lying on your back and getting fondled. Her hips beat a steady tattoo on his crotch.

Her hands pushed him to one side and tore at his fly, pulling the buttons open, working her hand inside until she closed around his erection. She gasped and gave one final shudder and went limp.

Before he could move away she was alert again. She pulled his penis from his pants and crooned to it.

"So beautiful. So marvelous! The best part of any man! And he's so huge! I just can't imagine anything that big finding room inside me . . . anywhere!" She bent and kissed the purple head, saw it jerk and laughed. "There's going to be a lot more of that, big guy. Just wait until we both get our clothes off."

She sat back and began working out of her dress, then the chemise and at last her drawers of white cotton that extended to her knee. Spur undressed as she did, sliding out of his boots, then out of the cheap black suit he had bought to

12

match his disguise as a salesman.

"You like big tits?" she asked Spur. "Big tits I got, maybe not a lot of brains, but in the tits department I win." She sat straighter and pushed her shoulders back, forcing her breasts forward until they hung like twin peaks, sagging only slightly from their size.

"This must be heaven," Spur said, bending to attend to them. He kissed each nipple, then worked a trail of kisses and tongue licks around each mount back to the peak. He was leaning in to reach her when her hand found his crotch.

"Christ, what a fucking fence post!" Jodi whispered. "No way that is going to fit either one of my hot holes."

"We can always try him for size," Spur suggested.

She pumped him six times. "If you don't, I'll chew him right down to the roots!"

Spur suddenly froze. He pulled her face up to look at him.

"Where is that other girl?"

"Why, ain't I enough for you? You need *two* cunts?"

"Who is she?"

"My sister. She's the shy one. We live here together. Why you worried about her?"

"She's not going to get the sheriff and bring him back and give him an excuse for hanging me?"

Jodi laughed. "Christ, no! She's out in the other room wondering what we're doing. And in another ten minutes she'll find her favorite candle and push it up her twat and candle fuck herself to

13

death. Don't worry about her. She's a little weird but harmless. Me, I'm just a clerk at the town's only good store. Hey, don't worry. This is the last place Sheriff Johnson would come looking for you. Believe me. Little sister Rebecca ain't going to the sheriff. We gonna talk about her all night?"

Spur showed her that they weren't. He lay on his back and pulled her on top of him. She dangled one breast after the other into his mouth. She fastened one hand on his crotch, massaging his balls tenderly, pumping him a half dozen times to keep on the edge.

She began trembling again. She wailed softly, got on her knees over him and lifted his sword straight up and lowered her scabbard around him until they were locked together.

"Oh, Christ, that *is* fine!" she crooned. "Damn, I've never been touched that deep before. You come half way out of my throat, I swear."

She shivered and then fell forward and rode him like a bucking bronco, bouncing and twisting, churning and turning him, putting more pressure and action on his lance than he had known for months.

He was gasping after the first twenty seconds. He saw sweat pop out on her forehead as she provided the motion, bucking and fucking him like a talented artist. He knew he was moving quickly down the path now. She was moaning and gasping with each lunge and twist.

Her hands were planted on his shoulders, then she dropped them to the bed beside him and the added thrust into her brought a soft scream of need, a demand for the ultimate fulfillment. She wailed again and her motions increased in speed and depth until they slammed together at the bottom of her stroke, sending shivers through their bodies.

Again and again and again they crushed their pelvic bones together until she was trembling and shrieking so violently that she couldn't maintain the riding motion.

She climaxed again and again, and Spur found himself over the edge, riding down the trail with only one ending. He was pounding upward now, unable to lie still when she ceased her motion, needing the surge of the pumping action to reach his glory land.

Sweat drenched both their bodies, their mouths hung open, gasping for air as Spur exploded and blasted his seed upward into her throbbing cavity.

She collapsed on top of him and they lay panting, sweat streaming off her body onto his. Neither could move. He heard the door open and wished he had the gun from his carpetbag. He didn't.

In the soft light of the lamp he saw the girl come in the door. She was the same one he had seen before, but now she wore a cotton flannel nightgown. She stared at the two bodies, moved on hand under the gown to her crotch and walked up beside the bed. She didn't look Spur in the eye. She watched for several minutes and he could see her hand moving. She gasped once, turned and went out of the room and closed the door.

Jodi sighed and pushed up so she could focus on Spur's face.

"That was my little sister, Rebecca. She's just curious."

"She's what twenty, twenty-one?"

"She twenty-two and I'm twenty-four and I'm still a virgin."

They both laughed.

"Rebecca has never been with a man?"

"True. No fucky-Becky. That's why she's curious. You'll have to show her what it's all about one of these nights, but not tonight. You're all mine."

She snuggled against him and Spur realized he had found a good information source. He could get started on his assignment tonight, after they settled down a little.

Spur McCoy was a U.S. Secret Service Agent. He stood 6-2, weighed 200 pounds, was 32 years old and had a full moustache, medium mutton chop sideburns that almost met his moustache, and a full head of brownish red hair.

He was an excellent horseman, a crack shot with derringer, six-gun and rifle, and kept in top physical shape at all times. He was an expert at hand to hand fighting as well as with knives and the staff.

He had come to this small Wyoming town in response to a Territorial representative to Congress who had complained about a sheriff in a northern county who had gone wild and set up his own little kingdom. Spur received the report through his boss, General William D. Halleck.

His job was to investigate the problem, and if practical, put an end to it. If that was not possible he was to call on troops from the nearest military post and settle the matter.

Usually he worked undercover, but this was so far away from the mainstream of western life, he figured that no one would have heard of Spur McCoy.

There was only one stage through town a week. He wanted to come in as low key as possible, and it was well he had. Anything else would have meant a shootout in the main street when he arrived. He figured he should be able to get a lot of good local information about the sheriff and his activities from Jodi. At least he had all night to work on it.

"You hungry?" Jodi said, sitting up, letting her fine breasts swing from side to side. She laughed. "Not these goodies, real food. Becky will be getting supper for us. She knows you will be hungry after your workout."

"Hungry—yes. First tell me about this sheriff. How does he expect anyone to stay in town when he meets them the way he did me?"

"You was big and looked able. So you was a threat to him. Little guys he don't work over so hard. He had a mean eye for you minute you lit from the rig."

"Does he own the whole town?"

"Mostly. We got a newspaper that tries to get the town to move, to get better. Little guy runs it. His name is Les Van Dyke. Been here three or four months. Bought the place sight unseen from

17

the other publisher who Sheriff Johnson ran out of town."

She jumped up, found her clothes and began dressing.

"Supper gonna be ready soon. You better get your pants on. Not that I'd mind you eating bare-assed. But Becky would be embarrassed."

He dressed. "The sheriff have everyone in town under his thumb? Isn't there anyone fighting him?"

"Yeah, a few, but they don't advertise. Biggest one right out in the open I guess is the Circle K. Big spread outside of town north called the Circle K run by Hans Klanhouser. He usually runs about ten thousand head and has from twenty to thirty hands, most of the time. Old Hans has more guns than the sheriff does if it comes to a range war."

"You're just full of good news."

She paused as she smoothed the chemise down over her breasts. "Why you so interested?"

"How can I sell my knives if this sheriff won't let me stay in town more than a week? I need more time than that to cover every business, every ranch, and every house in town. That's how I make my living."

"Oh, well, we'll buy something, you can bet on that. If the other samples are as good as the ones I saw in the case. I won't make any order though until morning, when I can figure out if the samples are good enough."

He swatted her on the bottom. She grinned and pushed her round cheeks out for him to swat

18

again. He did and she nodded and started to lift her skirts.

"Supper's ready." Becky called from the other side of the door.

Spur relaxed. He had a start on the assignment. He had found a playmate and now he was going to get supper. He opened the door for Jodi and they walked into the living room and kitchen of the small flat. A girl stood near the wood stove on the cooking side of the room. When she turned she glared at Spur and in her hand was a deadly little Adams pocket revolver with its ugly .32 caliber muzzle aimed directly at his chest!

CHAPTER TWO

Jodi froze for a second when she saw the gun, then she smiled.

"Well, Princess Rebecca, what have you fixed us for dinner, something just fine, I bet."

Spur took Jodi's lead. He grinned, nodded.

"Hi, Princess. Jodi tells me you're the best cook this side of the Mississippi! I'm Spur, you helped me out there in the alley when Sheriff Johnson bashed me. I just want to thank you a lot for helping me, Rebecca. Not everyone would come out there and help a stranger that way. I appreciate it."

The wild look in her eyes faded. The angry, dangerous expression melted from her face and her right hand slowly lowered the Adams. She was dressed the same way she had been in the alley, simple print, high around the throat, full skirt sweeping the floor.

Rebecca cocked her head to the side, blinked, and the start of a smile flickered across her face. It was gone, then came back and she put the pistol in a pocket somewhere in the big skirt. She smiled, bobbed in a try at a curtsy. She was prettier than her sister. Rebecca laughed and pointed at the big kettle on the stove.

"Stew, with a lot of vegetables and potatoes but not much meat, mostly left over rabbit from when I went hunting."

Jodi unfroze from her position and went to the stove.

"I'll help. You talk with our guest," Jodi said.

A few moments later they sat at the table. The stew was good and the bread thick and light. There was coffee and crabapple jelly. For dessert they had deep dish apple pie.

Spur sat back and reached for Rebecca's hand. She pulled it back.

"Princess, that was the best meal I've had in a long time. You should be cooking at the hotel or open a restaurant of your own somewhere."

"Oh, Mr. McCoy!" She turned, not able to hide her blush.

"Really, Rebecca," Jodi said. "It was a fine dinner. Thank you. Now, Mr. McCoy and I have to talk business. You understand, don't you,

22

Princess?"

"Yes." She didn't turn back.

Spur and Jodi went to the bedroom where she kissed him passionately.

"Eating always makes me feel sexy," she said.

"First, business," Spur said.

"Business?"

"Business. Who told you to watch for me at the stage? I saw you there when I got off."

She sighed, shook her head. "He said I wasn't supposed to tell anyone." Then she grinned. "But I guess that doesn't include you. His name is Lester Van Dyke. He runs the newspaper here. But you already knew that."

Spur relaxed. "Good. Now we're getting somewhere. What do you know about all this?"

"Only that Les complained to somebody and they told someone else and here you are. Federal lawman of some kind."

"And Sheriff Johnson always brings his new arrivals down this alley to beat them up?"

"Something like that." She unbuttoned the top of her dress, and he saw that she had nothing under it.

"That's a great pose, Jodi, but later. I have to see this Van Dyke as soon as possible. Where does he live?"

"Over the newspaper print shop."

"I'll find it." Spur reached for his hat, then cupped one of her big breasts through the open dress, bent and kissed it. "Delicious." He straightened and kissed her lips. "Now, what about Princess Rebecca?"

23

"Well . . . she has a few problems. But as far as I know she's been good as can be lately. I take care of her. She doesn't go out much, and never without me."

"How did it happen, her problem?"

"Our father was over-protective, over everything. Our mother died when Princess was born, and by the time she was ten, Pa was messing around with us. He'd get horny and need some and try, but I was twelve or thirteen and I'd tell him how bad he was and talk him out of it. I never had no idea he was messing with Rebecca.

"She never told me. I found out about that afterward. For three months he was having intercourse with her almost every night. She just kind of died inside. Then one night I caught them, and I hit Pa with a chair and ran him out of the house. I told Becky how ugly and evil it was and I guess I scared her. The next day she was sick and couldn't go to school and Pa came home early.

"I found them when I got back from school. We wasn't in this town then. The sheriff said Princess had been raped, so he knew. He didn't tell no one else but me. She killed Pa with a butcher knife when he was in her they figured. Then she pushed him off and kept stabbing and cutting and slashing. It was the most terrible thing I've ever seen. Blood all over the room, and it was hard to tell who he was. Wasn't nothing left between his legs at all.

"She's never been right since then. I wanted you to know."

"Thanks. Now, I better get a hotel room so the

sheriff can see me, and then I'll look up Van Dyke."

"You can stay here!"

"Then the sheriff would get curious. I better be more public." He bent and kissed one breast that peeked out of her dress. "I can't stay here, but I can spend some interesting nights here. Is there another entrance besides the alley?"

"No, I thought it would be safer this way for Princess."

He kissed her and took his gear out the alley door.

A half hour later he had registered in the Hotel Hartford, a rundown two-storey affair with twenty rooms and only six of them full. This was not a big tourist town.

He had little to unpack. For a moment he wasn't sure what to do with the six-gun and gun-belt, then he lifted the mattress and put them at the foot on top of the springs. A good search would find them, but he doubted if the sheriff was that interested in him just yet. Later he would be sleeping somewhere else. McCoy put a hideout derringer in his pocket. He left his suit on and walked into the crisp Wyoming night. The two saloons and gambling palaces in town were open and roaring.

He found the print shop and home of the *Wyoming Courier* in a small two-storey frame building that still had lights on. Spur tried the front door and found it unlocked. Inside he smelled that unique perfume of printers' ink mixed with newsprint that has a flavor like no other. To one side sat a desk and in front of it there was a long counter with banded sheafs of back issues of the paper. A man with a green eye-shade looked up, nodded, and waved Spur into the back room.

A press squatted in the middle of the floor with the printer's trade essentials grouped around it: boxes of flat paper, cases of type, cans of ink, and stacks of back records and old issues.

"Van Dyke?" Spur asked.

"Yes, did anyone see you come in?"

"I don't know. The sheriff didn't seem overly interested in me."

"Not after knocking you down. I saw you get off the stage."

"Like my performance?"

"Good enough so far. Do you know a general by the name of William D.?"

"Halleck is the last name of my boss. Was that the agreed on code and countersign?"

"Yes. Johnson will kill you if he knows who you are."

"How have you lasted so long here, Van Dyke?"

"I pretend to be a coward too. I print what he wants me to, but I'm about to change all that now that you're here."

"Don't be in a rush. Who can help us besides the Circle K?"

"Nobody. The banker in town is Otto Toller. He's weak, soft, and has his life's work and savings invested in this town. He wants to help us but he won't, he's too afraid."

26

Van Dyke sat down on a box of paper. "Hell, McCoy. I'm afraid too. Every dime I own is tied up in this paper. I paid fifteen hundred dollars for it, sight unseen, and without knowing a thing about the political situation. Now I'm in the middle of a county where the sheriff has just elevated himself to King and we all bow and scrape. That goes against my nature."

Van Dyke was five feet four inches tall, and slender. He had quick hands, a fertile and facile mind, and an enormous amount of drive and energy. He took off his spectacles and pinched his nose, then rubbed his forehead.

"Damned headache again." He looked up, small dark eyes evaluating McCoy. Van Dyke had a lean, whisker darkened jaw, a full moustache and dark hair that needed cutting. "What is your plan to put Sheriff Johnson in jail where he belongs?"

"I don't have one. I'm just trying to get my feet on the ground and find out what is going on. In jail? You have evidence that can convict him of a felony?"

"I can get it, plenty of it, when we have a safe situation for witnesses in this town. That won't be until after the sheriff is in jail or dead and his gunslinging deputies are jailed, shot or run out of town."

"He has it that tight?"

"He does. The only other man I would say just might help us is Nehemiah Hardy. Runs Hardy's Emporium. Biggest store in town and a damn fine man. He's level headed, a square shooter, and a

27

man I'd bank on if I needed help in a rush. But remember, he has a big investment here, too."

"I'll have a talk with him. Now, specifics. Is there one wide open case that we can work on to build up evidence of wrongdoing and hang it on Johnson? We'll need signed affidavits, hard evidence that can be backed up in court."

"Christ, there are so many."

"Evidence, we need hard, irrefutable evidence. Have there been any killings?"

Van Dyke laughed. "I've been here three months, and I have records showing that twelve men and one woman have been shot down in the streets. All by the sheriff or his deputies, and all 'in the line of duty'. How can you fight that?"

"We need just one flagrant case, one with witnesses that can prove the dead man was not armed, did not make any threatening moves, and show that the sheriff had serious, substantial and monetary ulterior motives for the killing."

"Like the county commissioner who tried to get Johnson recalled as sheriff. It would have worked, because women have the vote here, have ever since we became a territory back in sixty-eight. But the county commissioner wound up 'accidentally' dying in a fire that burned down his blacksmith and saddle shop. Happened late at night and nobody found him until the next morning. The sheriff certified it as an accidental death."

"This Sheriff Johnson covers his tracks?"

"Damn good. And he has three gunslingers he calls his deputies. I swear I had a wanted poster on one of them. But somehow it turned up missing from my stack."

"Hey, anybody home?" A booming voice came from the front of the office.

"I know that voice. Stay back here out of sight." Van Dyke went through the draped door into the office. Spur edged up to the fabric and looked through a crack along one side.

"Saw your lights on, thought I would check," the big man leaning over the counter said. He wore a leather vest with a silver star pinned to it.

Spur stared at the face. He had seen it before. Where?

"Just closing up. Need anything special?"

"Matter of fact, the sheriff gave me something for you. A guest editorial. Wants you to run it on the front page in your next issue. He's sure you'll cooperate. This is an important issue that affects the public safety." He put a sheaf of papers on the counter. "Here is it, not too long, but important. You take good care of it now, y'hear?" The man turned and headed out the door.

That was when Spur saw the scar down the deputy's right cheek. A three-inch curved scar. Spur tensed. He knew the man and he was positive the guy would recognize him. The deputy was Pete, Pistol Pete Bovert. Spur had helped put him away for ten years not too long ago in Arizona on a charge of multiple murder and rape.

Van Dyke went into the back. He made sure the deputy had left before he waved the pages of paper in an angry gesture.

"See what I mean? The man is smart, he

doesn't want to close me down, he wants to use me to cement his position. I'll be damned if I'm going to do it anymore!"

CHAPTER THREE

"Easy," Spur McCoy said. "I know you've been wanting to throw it in their faces, but not all at once. Fact is I know that deputy. Last time I saw him I was testifying against him in Yuma. He got five to ten at the Yuma Territorial prison. I'm going to have to work slow and careful on this and I want you with me, not dead in a gully somewhere."

"Goddamnit!" Les Van Dyke said, slapping his hand down on the box of newsprint. "I'm dying a little every day I have to knuckle under to these vermin. What was this guy's name when he went to prison?"

"Pete Bovert. The gang called him Pistol Pete because he always wore two of them and used them at the slightest excuse."

"Sounds familiar. Here they call him Pistol Pete, too, but his last name is Cody. Trying to sound Western I guess. He must have been the one I saw on the wanted poster."

"Where does this guy Hardy live? I need to talk to him, see what he knows, what he can do."

"I'll close up here and walk you over there and introduce you. He's a good man, but a little cautious. Hell, I'd be cautious too. He must have a twenty thousand dollar investment in this town."

Ten minutes later the men stood in the shadows in back of the Hardy house. Spur hadn't been inside, there was no way he could be tied to Hardy.

Nehemiah Hardy was a tall, slender man, with a gaunt, stubbled face, deep set eyes and a hawk nose. Fringes of black hair showed over his ears and around the back of his head. His eyes were quick and brown, and his handshake firm.

"Mr. McCoy, pleased to meet you."

"I'm glad. You might not be so happy once Les and I have had this little talk. I hope we can be friends, and work closely together. This is a problem for the whole county, and the leaders of the community must help."

"Well now, this sounds serious. Let me get a pint of cheer from the cellar and we can talk this over."

A half hour later Hardy shook his head. "Men, I appreciate you coming over, but it just won't work. Johnson has got everybody so tied in knots they don't know how to spit 'cept up wind. Nope, I'd say the only way to take care of the situation is like we used to in the army. When you got a sergeant who kept getting troops killed without cause, you just took care of him in the next little skirmish. Killed in the line of duty and that was it.

"Way I look at it, gents, the only way we can solve this here probelm is to put a bullet in fancy Mr. Sheriff Johnson and then run his riff-raff deputies out of the state."

"The West is coming of age, Mr. Hardy," Spur said. "We must uphold the law, use the law to take care of people like Sheriff Johnson. Which is precisely what we are going to do."

"Good luck. Hope it works." He paused. "Course now, you need a good rifle, I got some in stock, plenty of rounds. You just let me know. Got me some new Spencer seven shot repeaters, .52 caliber rim fire. Nice piece."

"I'll certainly keep that in mind, Mr. Hardy. Thanks for talking to us. This is all confidential, you understand."

They shook hands and Spur and Van Dyke headed back toward the newspaper office.

Rebecca sat in the main room of their small quarters and stared at the cross stitch design she worked on. Jodi was over at a "friend's" house. Rebecca was sure what Jodi was doing, but she would not think about that. Things like that should not be thought of by a good girl!

She needed to take a walk. It had been almost a month since she had taken a walk. This was a good time to do it since Jodi said she would not be home before midnight and told Rebecca not to wait up for her.

Rebecca told her that the book, the magazine and the cross stitch would be quite enough to keep her busy all evening. She smiled. Jodi didn't know everything.

She stood in front of the mirror by the door and studied her face. Yes, pretty, and her hair would be better when she combed it. Quickly she put on her best dress, and one with red and white figures on it. It was a little tight for her, but she managed to get the buttons over her breasts fastened. Yes, she looked nice.

She filled the pocket she had sewn in the long skirt of the dress as she usually did. Then she stood at the door leading into the alley until she saw someone stumble in and walk her way. Quickly she left the door and closed it. She walked slowly toward the figure who had lurched and stumbled forward. It was dark in the alley, but the moon had grown to half a round and smiled down on the hard packed earth.

Rebecca moved to the other side of the alley so she would meet the man who came toward her. She had never sen him before, and she knew he had been drinking. Fine, it didn't matter. He was a man, like the one she had seen today with his clothes all off lying under her sister who also was

34

naked.

Naked! A dirty word! She smiled. Dirty word!

The man stopped when he saw her coming. He looked up and she smiled. He was about thirty, maybe thirty-five, half drunk, taking a short-cut home. He didn't wear a gun, which was better. His brown hair spilled down over his forehead, and he brushed it back showing a two-day beard stubble and curious eyes.

"Well now, lookee here!"

"Hello, are you lonely?" Rebecca asked. She walked up until she could touch him and brushed her hand along his cheek. "You look lonely. Would you like me to be nice to you?"

"Keeereist, I must be drunk. I'm imagining you."

She caught his hand and put it on her breast. "No, you're not imagining it. I'm here. Let's sit down on those boxes over there and talk. I like your hand there. Does it feel good?"

"Oh, man, so pretty, and me drunk. Never too drunk for a good woman."

"Over here, and sit down. It's easier that way."

She led him to a place in the alley where one store was shorter than the rest and there was a twenty foot jog to its back door. A big packing crate lay there and she sat on it and waited for him to sit beside her.

Rebecca took his hand and put in on her breasts again, then she began unbuttoning the fasteners at her throat. A minute later he kissed her cheek, and he helped undo the buttons. He chuckled softly.

35

"Goddamn you are pretty! And you got big tits! My woman got little nubs. I'm feeling good. Gonna get it hard and everything! Damn, what a lucky night. Won twenty dollars at poker and now a beautiful fucking girl!"

The buttons were open to her breasts. He reached inside and caught her big orb. She wore no undergarments. Her breast popped out of the dress and he moaned in delight and bent to kiss it.

Rebecca had taken the butcher knife from the pocket she had made in her skirt. Using her right hand and gripping the knife like a club, with the point upward, she swung her right hand with all her might, aiming the tip of the twelve-inch blade for his stomach. The power of her swing drove the sharp blade through the man's thin shirt. The anger created the drive that plunged the knife into his belly just under the rib cage and sliced upward, penetrating his lung, then stabbing into his heart.

He rolled his eyes up at her in deadly surprise, before he collapsed away from her and rolled off the box. He lay on his back. He didn't move. Just like Pa. Good! He wouldn't hurt any more young girls. For a moment the man's face became that of her father.

Calmly she bent and pulled the knife from his chest, wiped the blood on his shirt until she was sure the knife was clean, then she put it safely in her skirt pocket and walked back to the unlocked door of her rooms, and slipped inside.

Rebecca washed the butcher knife carefully, dried it, and replaced it in the rack in the kitchen.

She was still awake and reading a book of poems by Edgar Allen Poe when Jodi came in. Her sister was used to Rebecca staying up until she got home, and she thought nothing of it. They talked about the poems and stories. Rebecca was not sure if she liked the *Cask of Amontillado* best of *The Tell Tale Heart*.

Jodi shrugged. Both of them were strange, vengeance-filled and bloodthirsty. But then Rebecca could be a little strange at times.

Back in the hotel room, Spur worked on his next course of action. He decided to give up on the knife selling guise. The deputy who knew him had ruined that plan. The first time Pistol Pete saw Spur he would reach for his gun. So Spur could get out of his city clothes and back to his jeans, shirt and brown vest.

He hadn't thought about the rancher yet. He could be a valuable ally if it came to a shootout. But Spur figured he should be able to handle this one without that kind of backing. His first project was to select one of the killings the sheriff himself had done, and start getting background on the man killed, and try to find some evidence of gain by the sheriff from the death.

He had to keep it as legal as he could and for as long as he could. Of course, if the other guys started shooting, he was more than ready to trade hot lead with them.

Spur got out his .44, a Remington New Model army six-gun he had picked up recently and found it balanced well for his kind of shooting. It had an eight inch barrel, five rifling grooves, an iron blade front sight and rear groove. It was blued, but worn some now and the varnished walnut grips were smooth. He cleaned the Remington, oiled it and loaded in five rounds, leaving the chamber under the hammer empty for safety's sake.

It was just after eight o'clock that Spur heard a knock on his door. He wasn't expecting company. In one fluid motion he picked up the .44, cocked the hammer with his thumb and flattened himself against the wall beside the knob side of the door.

"Yes, who is it?"

"A friend," a woman's voice said softly. Jodi? She wouldn't take that kind of chance. Curious, he unlocked the door and opened it slowly. No one came in.

He edged his eye around the door jamb and saw a girl of about seventeen standing in the hall. She wore a white blouse, long blue skirt and had black hair and dark eyes. She grinned at him and her eyes locked on his.

"Spur McCoy?" she asked, her voice teen-age thin.

"Yes."

"You must remember me from Denver."

He frowned, stepped out so he could get a better look at her. He saw her eyes appraising him from head to toe.

"Denver? No, I'm afraid not."

She darted into his room and closed the door, leaning against it.

"Of course you remember me. I'm the one with

a brown mole on my right breast. See." She opened her blouse, flapping it back to show her right breast where there was a mole.

"Miss, I've never been to Denver." He lied easily, worried what she might be a part of. She grinned, shrugged out of the blouse and laughed.

"So it was a way to get into your room. I was downstairs when you registered. I like you, like the tough smile, your moustache, the way you carry yourself. I've decided you are the man I want to . . . to deflower me, to take my virginity."

"That's flattering, Miss. But right now I have more important business. I have to. . . ."

"What's more important than taking a girl to bed, you know, fucking her?"

Spur laughed, picked up her blouse and handed it to her.

"What is more important is staying out of jail. Men get thrown into prison for just touching an underage girl like you. It's called statutory rape and it comes with a twenty year ticket. You should be worried about saving your virginity, not trying to get rid of it."

She ran to him, grabbed him around his back with her arms and pushed herself hard against his chest. She hung on, her head pressed into his shoulder.

She was crying when she looked up.

"You don't want me, you think I'm ugly. Even an ugly virgin should be a prize. Why won't you make love to me?"

She stepped back and began working at buttons on her skirt. He grabbed her hands.

"What's your name?"

"Violet."

He brushed the tears away from her face.

"Violet, you are a pretty girl. In another year or two you'll be a beautiful woman. Then you'll be glad that you still have your innocence. Some man will come along and be knocked out by you, and you by him. Hell, I haven't thrown a pretty girl out of my room for a long time, but I'm going to tonight. Now you put your blouse back on and button it, or you're going into the hall bare breasted. Do you want that?"

She pulled his hand up to her breasts but he moved it away.

"No tricks. Out you go."

He held one wrist, pulled her to the door and then pushed her into the hall. He threw her blouse after her and closed and locked the door quickly. He had seen no one in the hall. He listened for a minute, heard her sigh and then footsteps down the hall going away. He shook his head. That was one problem he really didn't need.

When Spur decided she had left, he put the room's only wooden chair under the door handle, bracing it so anyone coming into the room would have to break the chair first. Then he looked at the bed and tested it. Hard, lumpy, but softer than the floor.

Spur took out his carpetbag and checked the contents, then found the badge he had been sent. It was a shield with the U.S. seal on it and the words: U. S. Secret Service. It was new. Each officer was supposed to carry one. In undercover

40

work, Spur was relieved of that duty. He took his badge and the thin leather folder they had made for it, and opened the false bottom section of his carpetbag. It came unhinged on the side of the bag when he pressed a small trigger set into the outside of the base of the bag. In the small compartment, a half inch deep and six inches square, he put the badge and a card that could also identify him. Already in the compartment were five one-hundred dollar bills. He had forty dollars in his wallet, and one hundred dollar bill in a hard to find section.

Spur had just put everything away and stretched out on the bed wondering what he could do that night. For a moment he froze thinking about Pistol Pete. Then he relaxed. He had been using a cover name on that Arizona operation. Pete would not recognize his real name. So all he had to do was stay out of sight when the deputy was around.

Five minutes later, as Spur was deciding if he wanted to go to bed, someone pounded on the door.

"Open up, McCoy. This is the sheriff."

Spur caught up his six-gun and held it behind his hip as he moved the chair.

"Yes, just a minute, I'm coming."

He unlocked the door and as he did it was kicked forward.

Spur stared into the angry face of Deputy Sheriff Pistol Pete Bovert who had both hand guns aimed at Spur's chest.

"Sure as hell! When Sheriff Johnson described

41

you, I was sure as shit that it was you. Welcome to Wyoming, Spur McCoy, or Sam Martin as we called you in Yuma. As the Indians say, this is a good day for you to die!''

CHAPTER FOUR

Spur looked at the twin deathbringer .44 muzzles and chuckled.

"Yes, I can see we have an efficient sheriff's department in this county. I was wondering when you might come by looking for your free knife. It is my extreme pleasure to facilitate such a small benevolent contribution to the law enforcement personnel of the county. If, my good man, you will step this way I'll be glad to show you the latest in fine cutlery, and you may make the selection of your choice. Oh, of course, with no charge to a lawman. I didn't quite catch what you said about Yuma or that other name, but no matter. Would you like to see something in a skinning knife, or perhaps a matched set of steak knives?"

Spur hoped to catch Pete completely off guard. He did with his spiel. He ignored the guns and managed to hide his own Remington behind his hip as he led Pistol Pete to the bed where the sample case still lay open.

Pistol Pete never had been long on brains. He turned and looked at Spur again.

"Goddamn! Swear you was the same hombre that fried my ass in Yuma and put me in the Territorial. Hell, I busted out after six months. Got me a couple of them fucking guards in the break!" He stared at Spur. "You sure you ain't been in Yuma? You was some kind of federal marshal or special agent or some damn thing back then."

"My good man. I came here directly from Boston and the Boston Knife Works, probably the best cutlery makers in all of the nation. We have excellent knives for commerce, for the house, and even for fighting."

Spur watched as Pistol Pete shoved both hog legs into leather and looked at the knives. Spur picked up a six-inch bladed hunting knife and began talking about it. Then he gave a small demonstration how it could be used for slashing, stabbing, skinning or almost any frontier use.

"Notice how the tip is Bowie sharpened. Cuts both ways." Spur flicked the blade and sliced a two-inch wound on Pistol Pete's right arm.

"What the hell?"

Spur pulled up his left hand which held his own
.44.

"Bovert, you filth! You could have at least had
the brains to change all of your name."

The Deputy backed to the door, his hands
poised over his six-guns.

"Right, get rid of them before I have to shoot
you in the balls and watch you cry. You want to
cry, Bovert? You want to cry and beg for mercy
the way you made that Indian girl do before you
raped and then multilated her?"

"God, you *are* McCoy!" His hands twitched
over his guns. "I should have shot first and then
talked. Damn it!"

"Take the right hand six-gun out by your
thumb and finger, easy, and put it on the floor.
Then do the same thing with the other one."

"No. I don't give up my guns."

"Then you die where you stand. Take your
choice. You have five seconds. One . . . Two . . .
Three . . ."

Pistol Pete lifted the weapons and put them on
the floor.

"Man to man, McCoy. You and me, each with
one of them knives right here! I'll take you on."

"Yes, you probably would, if I gave you the
chance. Too many men have given you that
chance. How many men and women have you
killed now, Pete? Twenty, thirty? And most of
them when they were unarmed. Remember the
rancher and his wife? They just got in your way.
But you raped the woman and made her husband

45

watch. Then you sliced them into pieces with your knife. You're a dead man, Pete. The law will get you one way or the other. If prison didn't work, the equalizer will. A .44 slug judiciously applied works wonders."

Pistol Pete charged. Spur had hoped he would. The Secret Service man slashed with the knife, laying open a wound across Pete's chest to draw his attention. Then Spur clubbed the big man with the butt of his pistol just hard enough to put him down and unconscious.

McCoy rolled over the big form, stopped the flow of blood and tied him hand and foot, then he waited. By midnight there would be fewer people around the hotel and on the streets.

Spur dozed off on the bed, woke up when Pistol Pete began kicking his boot heels against the wooden floor. Spur hit him with a pillow and he stopped. It was 2:00 A.M. when Spur pulled on his boots and strapped on his six-gun. He checked the hall and saw no one there.

McCoy knelt beside Pistol Pete. "See this derringer? It's a .45 and it will be buried in your gut. I'm going to untie your hands and feet and help you walk out to the street. You so much as blink crooked or make a sound, and I'll blow your belly full of lead, you understand?"

"Yeah, McCoy. And I understand that you're a dead man. No way I'm not coming after you."

"There's one way, dead. And you remember that."

They met no one going down the back stairs to the alley. Once there Spur marched the deputy to the next street and through the next block to the edge of town.

"Keep walking, killer," Spur told Pete. "You and me are going to have a little talk out here away from town."

"I'll take you on anywhere, McCoy."

They walked for twenty minutes, through a shelf of land and down toward the Greybull River. The farther they walked the more nervous Pete became.

"What the hell you looking for?" Pete screamed. "Nothing out here but some cattle and some worked out mines."

"Sounds good," Spur said. He had out his six-gun now as he had for the past mile.

Without warning Pete began to run. He sprinted for a ledge and dove over it. By the time Spur got to the top, Pete was still rolling toward the water at the bottom of the wash.

Spur shot twice. He saw the first slug tear into Pete's legs. The second took him just below his navel and plowed a bloody, dirty track through his intestines and slammed out his back not far from his backbone.

Spur walked down the slope easily, watching in the half moonlight, the figure on the dry grass near the edge of the water.

"Oh, goddamn!" Pistol Pete said. He repeated the phrase a dozen times, then saw Spur standing over him.

"Gut shot me, you bastard!"

"Seems I remember hearing how you gut shot a woman and two kids in a store in California. Sat

47

there and watched all three die."

"Bastard!"

"It's different when you're on the other end of the hot lead, isn't it, Pete?"

"Dirty bastard!"

"What can you tell me about Johnson? I came after him, you're just a bonus. You might as well even out the score a little. Where is Johnson weak? Where should I attack him?"

"Go fuck yourself!"

"Figure you have another half hour to live, Pete. Maybe an hour if you're unlucky. Hurts like hell, doesn't it? Just try to think about all those people you slaughtered. About that old Breed woman you tied to her rocking chair and then burned her shack down around her. You didn't leave until she stopped screaming. Think about that, Pete." ·

"McCoy! Don't make it happen this way. End it for me now! I can't stand it any more!"

"Where is Johnson weak?"

"Women, damnit! He's a cockhound. Tease him with a good woman and he'll jump through a hoop. Now do it! I can't stand the pain! Do it right . . ."

Spur's .44 blasted a hollow hole in the northern Wyoming wilderness. Society had been relieved of one of its failures. The sound echoed and echoed again and again down the sleek flow of the Greybull River, rolled up the banks and washed out over the plateau until it was ground into dusty sound particles which scattered into the winds of Wyoming's night.

Pete Bovert slammed forward, a small hole in the base of his skull. He flopped on his face inches from the water. Spur rolled him over and pushed him into the fast flow of the water which moved away from the town of Elk Creek. It would be better if the body were not found for a few days. After that it shouldn't make any difference.

Spur held the Remington for a minute, then pushed it into his holster and watched the body sliding away downstream. He had been an executioner tonight. He didn't mind. It had been a miscarriage of justice when Bovert had been given a jail sentence in Yuma. He should have been hung. Spur was only carrying out the just intent of the law. No animal like Bovert should be allowed to grow up, let alone carry a lawman's badge.

Women! So the high and mighty sheriff was a glutton for women. Maybe Jodi could help him out some way—but not if she would be in any danger. He would work on the idea, keep it as a last resort.

Spur walked back to town, slipped into the hotel when no one was watching the back door, and got into bed. He locked the door and braced a chair under the handle, then went to sleep. His .44 was beside his right hand. He lay on his back, fully clothed and with his boots on. He would sleep on his back, and be alert at the slightest sound. After tonight he would not be able to sleep in the hotel, because he was sure the sheriff would be looking for him.

* * *

49

Spur came awake at dawn. He stretched, got up and changed clothes, putting on his jeans and shirt, brown vest and his brown hat. Then he packed his belongings, took the bag and his knife sample case and slipped out of the hotel. He had to knock twice on the door in the alley behind Main Street before Jodi came to open it. She grinned when she saw him.

"One hell of a time to come calling. Want some breakfast?" She was still half asleep. He put her back in bed, kissed her forehead and she was sleeping again.

Spur left his bags in the big living room-kitchen, and when he turned around he found Rebecca dressed and alert, eyes sparkling as she nodded a shy good morning. Spur watched her light a fire in the small wood range and make breakfast. He tried to talk to her, but she would only smile, answering questions with a shake or nod.

In ten minutes she had breakfast for him: scrambled eggs, hash browns, three strips of thick bacon, toast and coffee. She ate as he did. He noticed that she wore an old, faded dress that was slightly large for her, conveniently hiding almost all signs of her breasts or her waist.

"Thank you, Rebecca. I have to do some things this morning. The sheriff will be looking for me today. Would it be all right if I stayed here tonight? I can sleep on the floor somewhere."

"That would be fine, Mr. McCoy," she said. "I'll tell Jodi so she'll know too."

"Thanks, Rebecca. That was a fine breakfast."

50

He reached out to touch her hand, but she pulled it back quickly.

She nodded, mumbled something and her hand snaked into the pocket she had sewn into the full skirt.

Spur went to the door, checked the position of his six-gun, waved at Rebecca and went into the alley. He walked quickly to the alley in back of the newspaper office, found the right door and stepped inside.

The rear door was unlocked. Spur almost called out so he wouldn't get shot as a prowler. But he heard voices coming from the front. Without a sound, Spur made his way past the press toward the draped doorway. The voices came stronger now.

"Look, you little shit head! I don't care if you disagree with what I have to say or not. You goddamn well better run it on the front page with my name on it, or I'm gonna run your skinny little ass right out of town. Do I make myself clear?"

Spur didn't recognize the voice. The next one he knew at once: it was Les Van Dyke.

"Sheriff, I've been pressured to run stories before, but nobody in his right mind ever threatened me like that. I'd say you are in one hell of a lot of trouble. We do have a territorial government, you know. And laws. And right now I could charge you with three or four different felonies. I'm sure you know all this. You just don't quite understand that you aren't the king of Elk Creek anymore."

"I'm not, huh? We'll see. You run the goddamn story or we'll fucking well see!"

"You kill me, who is going to set the type and run the press? You think about that for a while."

The shot came almost at once. Spur drew his gun and pulled back the drape so he could see into the office.

CHAPTER FIVE

When Spur McCoy heard the shot he peered through the curtained door into the front of the newspaper office. Sheriff Johnson lowered his gun. A few pieces of the big window in front of the office had fallen to the floor from the shot the lawman had sent into it. Johnson laughed, stepped through the jagged glass onto the boardwalk and walked down the street.

"Damnit! I'm going to send a bill to the county!" Van Dyke yelled through the window toward the retreating lawman. "Christ, what a mess!"

"Van Dyke, it's McCoy in the back room," Spur called. "The door was open. I heard. This seems like a bad time to come calling."

Van Dyke didn't reply. Two people came to stare in the window. "Yes, I know it's broken," he said to them, and picked up a broom and a cardboard box and went outside to clean up the glass. "Talk to you when I get back inside," he said as he went past the draped doorway of the printing plant.

Spur waited. He thought at first that he could glean important facts from back issues of the newspaper about some of the killings, or just one target murder. But he quickly discounted that. Johnson would reveal nothing important about any of the deaths, and if Van Dyke found out any incriminating evidence, he wouldn't be able to print it anyway.

But Van Dyke would know which of the killings would be the easiest to prove as murder against the sheriff and his deputies. The hired deputies undoubtedly pulled the trigger. When they did it was on orders of the sheriff, so he had conspiracy, as well as a murder charge against the sheriff.

Ten minutes later Van Dyke came back inside for some boards to cover the broken window. It measured six feet square and he said it would take him three months to get another piece of glass that big from Cheyenne.

"I've been thinking about the best murder to pin on the sheriff," Van Dyke said when he had the boards in place. "Have to be Adam Fowler. He got shot from ambush about three weeks ago.

54

The word was that his wife had been friendly, shall we say, with the sheriff, and Adam went to settle up with him. Adam Fowler was the only preacher we had in town.''

"Interesting. Fowler wound up shot in the back?''

"How did you know?''

"A specialty of Pistol Pete. What else do we have?''

"Not much. The widow is still in town. Staying at the parsonage, being supported by the community church. She's been carrying on, crying and weeping, but nobody believes much of it. From what I hear, the lady still sees the sheriff.''

"Tell me where I can find the widow,'' Spur said. "I should pay my respects.''

"I also hear that she is the best spy the sheriff has to the goings on around town. So be careful of Kate Fowler.''

A half hour later Spur knocked on the back door of the Community Church parsonage at the north end of the little town. At first there was no reaction. After a second knock he heard a sound, then a voice asking him to wait a minute. Two minutes later heels clicked on hardwood floors as someone came to the door. It opened.

The woman who stood looking at him was tall, five eight at least. She wore high heels and a black dress that clung tightly to her upper body, nearly bursting at the bodice and pinched in at her tiny waist, then flaring over hips into flounces of four different colors. It was a dance hall girl's dress.

"Hello. Who are you? You're not from the church committee. You're staring, did you want something?"

Spur laughed. "Yes, I'm Spur McCoy, are you Kate Fowler?"

She nodded. Her clear brown eyes were unblinking. She had her dark hair piled on top of her head and the dress was cut low showing half of each white mound of breast.

"I'd like to talk to you a few minutes."

She smiled, and Spur enjoyed the picture. "You're the new man in town, on the stage yesterday and already our sheriff doesn't like you. Come in, come in. I was trying on costumes that someone left. This is a snazzy one, don't you think?"

"It looks perfect on you, if you're working a saloon."

"You don't think I could?"

"Kate, I expect that you may have. You certainly have a full, provocative body."

She glowed at the praise. "Well, thank you. I like you. I can tell you're a man with a lot of potential. I like my men big. I mean most men are proportionally large all over. It's a kind of hobby of mine."

"Interesting hobby."

"True. You said you had some questions?"

"Yes. I'm here to find out who killed your husband and why."

They were in the kitchen of the small house, and she waved him into the living room, then on to her bedroom. The bed had not been made, and clothes lay scattered around the room. She didn't apologize, just reached to the dresser where she picked up a hand rolled cigarette, and lit it with a stinker match.

"The why is the easy part. He thought I was stepping out on him, making love with another man."

"Were you?"

She laughed. "In four months you're the first person who has ever had enough guts to come right out and ask me. The answer is yes. But not who he thought."

"Did your lover kill your husband?"

"Hardly. We were in bed with each other at the time."

It was Spur's turn to chuckle. "You seem to be an extremely honest, straightforward person, Kate."

"I know what I like." She smiled and looked Spur up and down. "The more I see and hear of you, Mr. McCoy, the more I like."

"I was about to say the same thing."

"You haven't seen much of me yet."

"I can always hope." He moved toward her. She waited. He leaned in and kissed her cheek, then her lips. She backed off and shook her head.

"Not right. I'd need a dozen or more that way to decide. Let's sit down and figure out if we enjoy that or not."

She sat on the edge of the bed and Spur dropped beside her.

"First, undo some of those buttons up the back of this dress. It's so damn tight it hurts."

Spur unfastened all the buttons and she held the dress on with her arms as he leaned in to kiss her again. This time they both had their lips parted and their tongues wandered lazily in and out of each other's mouths.

"I think I like that," she said as they came apart.

"I know I like it," Spur said. He nibbled at her lips then kissed her again and eased her backward onto the bed.

"Now you're getting serious. I'm a girl who can't think well lying on her back."

"You don't have to do any thinking," he said.

She kissed him again. Spur took the top of the dress and pulled it down. Her breasts tumbled out like two ripe melons.

He teased them with feather touches until she moaned in delight.

"How did you know I love it that way?" she asked. "Yes, sweetheart, yes!"

He touched them more and then massaged them delicately before he bent down and kissed each straining nipple.

"Oh nice, nice. Love that almost as much as fucking."

Spur spread her legs with his knee and lay directly on top of her, his body pressing down hard on her crotch. He kissed her breasts again, then her lips.

"So you were fucking the sheriff's brains out when he had your husband gunned down?"

"Christ, don't ask now!"

"Now is when I'm asking. You were with him?"

58

"Yes, yes!"

"And the sheriff told one of his men to blow your husband into heaven or hell. Which man did he tell?"

"Somebody in the hall."

"And you'll testify in court you heard him say the words."

"No. Tyler would cut my tits off if I did that! You know he would."

"Not if Tyler Johnson was in a jail cell."

"He ain't."

Spur pulled up her long skirt and his hand worked between her legs.

"Oh, lordy but that feels good! You've got a gentle way with a woman, Spur. Most men would have pumped off and had their pants back on by now."

"The second time will be fast and hard."

"Just keep it hard!" She found his penis and rubbed it through his pants. "Get him out for me."

"You're not ready yet," he said. Spur sat up, stripped out of his vest and shirt, then pulled off her skirt and her drawers. They were made of soft silky material, the same knee length as most women wore. As he pulled them down over her little belly, she moaned. Then he began kissing them down to her crotch, kissing around the hairy pubis and on down her inner thigh.

Kate Fowler jerked and moaned and writhed all the way.

"Hurry, lover! I want you inside of me right now. Please hurry. I'm all wet and swollen and

59

ready. Please get in me right now, Spur! I need you in me."

"Which deputy was it Johnson told to kill your husband?"

"Christ! What difference does it make? He's dead. But I'm alive. I won't be if I keep talking about the sheriff. Christ, Spur come on, fuck me!"

His finger found her secret place and he rubbed. She jolted with one spasma of joy and then he withdrew. "Which one was it, Kate?"

"Hell, what does it matter? It was Pistol Pete. And that's all I know. I was busy, after that. Now, Spur, let's make it one to remember."

Spur stripped off his pants and underdrawers, then moved between her legs and worked into her slowly. She climaxed before he was settled, and then again. He knew he had a problem with Pete being dead. Still he could prove conspiracy to murder, and also a charge of murder. If the woman's testimony would hold up. It wouldn't. A defense attorney would have a circus with her on the stand. And he had no witnesses to prove that Pete pulled the trigger on the Reverend Mr. Adam Fowler. It had been a good try, a close miss. However, in any court action he could call on the woman as a witness to show general, if not specific, misconduct. That would help.

Spur was thinking more about the girl under him now than the job. She was an exciting combination of good looks, good body and absolute wanton desire. How could she miss? He came away from her suddenly. She had already climaxed four times.

"Get up on your hands and knees," he told her.

"Oh, no!"

"Oh, yes!"

Spur mounted her from behind, driving into her still pulsating vagina with one solid thrust and she looked over her shoulder at him.

"Oh, there!"

But Spur was too busy to notice. He had slid over the last ridge and began the long ride down through the chute, around the corners and slamming into the open with the speed of a runaway railway locomotive. He was pounding and shaking and shouting. He felt and heard her doing the same as they climaxed together and fell on the bed in a tangle.

Five minutes later after they had recovered enough to talk, she grinned and played with the hair on his chest.

"Not bad for a preacher's widow, right?"

"You weren't always a preacher's woman."

"True. Adam 'saved' me from my life of sin. He pulled me out of a whorehouse in Arizona and brought me up here to reform, reeducate, and religionize me. He called them my own kind of the three R's. It didn't work. But then he only had a little under a year to work on me. Hell, I just like to fuck. I don't see what's so wrong doing it. Who gets hurt? Did I hurt you? Hell no! Made you feel damn fine there for a few minutes. How can that be bad?"

"There are other considerations," Spur said.

"Not for me. I got sick when I was thirteen. German measles or something like that. Anyway, it killed me as a mother. No kid is ever gonna stick his head out of my crotch and scream. My insides are all sick. Doctor didn't tell me why, just said I couldn't never have none."

"At least you aren't bitter."

"How can I get mad at the measles?"

"But you can get mad at Tyler Johnson. He's had as many as a dozen men killed in this county. Does that mean anything to you, Kate?"

"Yeah, sure, it's wrong. And one woman he killed I know of. I don't want Kate Fowler to be the second one."

"When it gets that far, when we have enough evidence to arrest him, we'll shut down his deputies too, and he won't have a chance to hurt anyone."

"Then you got yourself a witness."

"It won't be long."

She reached for his crotch and found him limp.

"Hey, what about that second fast and furious one you promised me?"

"Give me a minute to catch my breath. I need to know who else in this town can help me nail Sheriff Johnson inside his own jail house."

She talked about half the people in town, but none of them seemed right. Spur was stalling. In college once he had made love to three different girls in an hour on a bet.

He won the bet and spent his winnings sending the loser to a bawdy house for the night. Now he needed a half hour between go-rounds.

Kate stopped talking and bent to his crotch. In a moment she had him in her mouth coaxing him until her ministrations resulted in his total firmness. She looked up and smiled.

"Do you mind? I haven't tasted any in so long."

He growled at her as she went down on him and Spur lay there delighted and fascinated. Somehow he never had any staying power when a beautiful woman began sucking on him. He didn't this time. It was less than two minutes until he was shouting and moaning and clawing the air as he climaxed in a bursting surge of powerful feelings that left him at once drained, and curiously, hungry.

She slid away from him and grinned. "You just don't know all the talents I have. What's for number three?"

Spur began pulling on his clothes. "Number three is for me to get back to work."

Spur turned. "Someone is knocking on your front door."

She jumped up, pulled on a robe and looked through the hallway at the glassed front door.

"God, get your clothes on fast, it's Sheriff Johnson and he looks madder than all hell!"

CHAPTER SIX

Nehemiah Hardy gave Jodi her week's wages. Jodi was the best retail person he had ever hired for the store, man or woman. She had taken over the housewares and house supplies sections and done the ordering and most of the selling. That left him time to take care of the rest of the store, the hardware, fencing, barbed wire and the rest of the man-related items. Now he wasn't sure he could run the store without her.

"Thanks, Jodi, for another week of good work. I'm glad you're here."

"So am I Mr. Hardy. I don't know what

Rebecca and I would do without you." She touched his hand. "We appreciate it."

Something flared deep in his loins but he swept it away.

"Goodnight, Jodi," he said firmly.

She smiled and went out the door locking it behind her.

Nehamiah turned down the last lamp and went into the back room to work on the books. He was making money, not a lot but enough to live on comfortably. That word reminded him of the ranch. He should go out and check on everything. He tried to get out there once a month, but it was hard. He knew it would be tough sometimes, but he had gone ahead. At times he told himself he had no choice. He had been young and not as smart as he was now.

So long ago. Nehemiah Hardy let the years wind back to the day he arrived in the county fresh from Boston. He had ridden a horse in from Casper so he could see some of the country. That last night outside of town he had camped by the Greybull River and early in the morning had gone for a walk. He wasn't the only one up. Two women were bathing and splashing in the cool waters of the river. One dressed and left hurriedly, but the other, the younger one stayed.

Hardy had grinned and slipped up as close as he could. Then he could see that she was an Indian. He had no idea what tribe, but he figured she was about sixteen. She had a slender young body, full hips and small breasts that kept him in a constant state of excitement.

She washed herself again, then sat in the sun to dry and made no attempt to cover her young and tempting body. At last he could stand it no longer and rose and walked toward her. She was not surprised. She had known he was watching and had waited for him. She stood and turned slowly so he could see her, then cupped her breasts in her hands and walked slowly toward him.

He had no idea what it meant, but when she pulled him down in the grass, he knew what she wanted. They made love in the grass all morning until he was absolutely limp beyond recall. Hardy was mesmerized. Never had he made love so long, or so gloriously. She did anything he wanted her to.

She knew two words of English: *You stay*. He did, for a week, making love every morning until he was exhausted, then they worked together at a small lean-to she had fashioned in a bend of the river where a blush of green trees came down to the water. She had only the most primitive clay pots and no metal tools or utensils at all.

He stayed another week, watching her hunt rabbits, and pheasant. He was curiously contented. Then he remembered his business waiting for him in Elk Creek. It had been a family business that one of his uncles began years ago. Now the man wanted out, and offered it to Hardy at a pittance but enough for the old man to live on back in Boston.

Hardy had started calling the slender Indian, *Girl*, and the name stuck. He explained to her with signs that he would return, that he had to go to

Elk Creek. She had communicated to him that it was a half day's ride to the town.

Hardy promised he would come back with pots and cooking things. She wept and wailed, tore off her fringed buckskin dress and beat her fists on the ground. At last he rode away.

The store had been everything his uncle promised. The older man stayed two weeks, getting Hardy familiar with the business, the merchandise, his set of books, and the various wholesale houses he ordered goods from. It was another two weeks before Hardy thought of Girl. He closed the store late Saturday night, loaded up a pack horse with two big sacks of kitchen and cooking gear, blankets, and some ready to wear clothes he thought might fit her, and rode for the camp.

That Saturday night he had missed the bend in the river, and by morning was lost. He came back down the river and at last found the bend, and where her camp had been, but she wasn't there. He searched until almost dark before he found her in another cope of woods back from the stream. She did not believe that he had returned.

To greet him she at once made love with him in the grass, then she looked at all the things he had brought to her. She wept with joy. Never had she had a metal pot to cook in. She was so delighted he couldn't stop her tears.

That night, and all day Monday he stayed. He taught her the first words of English, *Go, come back, Girl, Hardy.* He told her to stay at that spot, he would build her a log house. Then at mid-

68

night he left again, promising that he would come back and this time she believed him.

Gently Hardy probed the locals how they felt about squaw men, and got quick and hostile reactions. Then he knew he had to keep his Indian woman a secret.

The first four months he managed to get out to see her every other Sunday. He told people who asked that he went fishing and hunting up the Greybull. They believed him. What else was there to do in the wilderness?

On the first visit he made in August of that year he saw that she was pregnant. Girl was pleased. She jabbered at him excitedly. He slowed her down and they used English and some words of Sioux. She belonged to a split off tribe of the Teton Sioux, but few of her people remained.

On each visit he learned more Sioux words and she learned more English. Two trips later he found an older woman living there and Girl said she was her mother. She stayed. Before winter he had built a twelve foot square log house. He had it roofed by the time the snows fell, and with the snows came a one-eyed brave. Girl said he was One-Eye, her brother. He had a squaw and built a lodge in the deepest part of the woods. During the heavy snows that winter One-Eye and his squaw lived in the cabin.

In February, Hardy's son was born, and he brought a small wood stove to the cabin, and a month later a wood burning range with eight lids.

With the coming of spring Hardy bought six calves, five heifers and one good bull for his ranch. Now most of the town knew he had a ranch out there, and that he used Indians to run it for him, and if the people thought that strange, they didn't say so.

He found out the land was available and home-steaded his 160 acres. A year later he had a daughter with blue eyes like her brother. The herd had grown to twelve due to some strays One-Eye had collected. None of them had brands. Hardy made up his own brand, Bar H, but never registered it.

A year later Hardy met Wendy, who played the pump organ for the church services. She had long blonde hair and fair skin and the bluest eyes he had ever seen. She was only five feet tall, and so pretty it made his chest burst just thinking about her. He was so much in love he dreamed about her day and night. He wanted to be around her con-stantly. He went places he knew she would be so he could see her, listen to her talk, let her look at him and sometimes talk with her. Nothing like this had happened with Girl. He had simply made love to her and lived with her.

With Wendy it was different.

Wendy would not permit him to touch her except hold her hand on special occasions. He asked her father permission to court her and at last won his approval. It was a nine month court-ship. Nehemiah was seven years older than the seventeen year old Wendy.

She was the perfect lady, allowing him to touch her, to put his arm around her, and at last, after they had decided that they would get married and

he had her father's blessing, she let him kiss her
. . . once.

Wendy had been a perfect wife and mother.
They had four strong, happy children, and he
never breathed a thought about his Indian family
to her. His visits became less frequent to his
ranch. He herd grew and at last the railroad went
through and they could take some of the cattle to
the railroad at Rawlins.

Hardy hired two out-of-work cowhands to help,
and he got on a horse with them and with One-
Eye they drove a hundred head to the pens. That
year they got twenty dollars a head for the cattle,
and after Hardy paid off the drovers he still had
$1,800. He set up a bank account for One-Eye,
bought him a new saddle, a dozen blankets, and a
rifle he had been wanting. He split the profit in
the middle, and told Girl the rest of the money
was for her and the children. She wept. She didn't
know what to do with it. Hardy said to keep it for
the children.

Now his Indian children, Adam and Beth, were
13 and 14 years old. He wanted them to come to
the town school, but he knew that was not possible. Maybe in fifty years it would be. He took
them books and primers and taught them to
speak English, but it was hard at long range.

Now, Nehemiah Hardy looked at his ledger
books. He would clear more than three thousand
dollars again this year. He could live on six
hundred a year. The profit went into his cousin's
bank in Boston where he now had a balance of
over $65,000. It was truly a fortune. His local

bank account was for the day to day running of the business. He didn't trust Otto Toller with a lot of money—and there were no guarantees.

His account for Adam and Beth had soared to nearly ten thousand dollars. The ranch was flourishing. He had hired a white manager, with the understanding that the Indians be left alone, and be provided for. They had built a new ranch house, and barns and outbuildings. It was a real ranch. Yearly they drove cattle to the railyards, sometimes as many as three hundred.

Hardy closed the books and turned out the last lamp. He walked to the front door in the dark, unlocked it and stepped out.

"Hold it right there!" A voice snapped. Hardy heard a six-gun cock.

"It's all right, Sheriff. I own the place. Hardy."

"Good," Sheriff Johnson said. "Just the man I want to see. Feeling is running high against the Injuns again. You hear the talk. I figure we better clear all the Sioux out of the county. You got four or five savages on your little ranch. You better get rid of them for their own safety."

"No, Sheriff. I don't think that's necessary. People around here know the Indians on my ranch. They seldom leave it, and I see no problem."

"Didn't ask you if you saw a problem, Hardy. I said move them savages out of there before I have to go out there with a posse and shoot them out."

"Sheriff. You don't have that kind of authority. Your job is to uphold and enforce the law. There

72

is no law against Indians living in this county. There couldn't be, it would be unconstitutional.''

"That's what I figured.''

"What did you figure?''

"That you're nothing but a goddamn squaw man. I done me some inquiries of my own. Them savages been on that land for fifteen years now. Lived there before you homesteaded. And you built that first little cabin on that place fourteen years ago. Just in time for the first brat that young squaw dropped. To me that makes you a squaw man, Hardy.''

"Sheriff, you are entitled to any personal opinion you want. Personally I think you're a poor sheriff, but until I bring you up on some kind of specific charges, it's just my opinion. My advice to you, sheriff, is to stick to law, not opinion, it's a lot safer.''

Sheriff Johnson bristled when Hardy began, then he burned silently until the store keeper was through.

"Hardy, you interest me. I'm going to dig a little deeper, find out more about your nest of savages out there. And when I do, I'll be paying you a visit, a damn interesting visit. Because then I'll have facts and witnesses and evidence that you're not going to like at all!''

The sheriff spun on his boot heel and marched away. Hardy took a deep breath. he didn't want to hurt Wendy. If she knew about Girl and the two kids out there it would break her heart. She had been a perfect wife. He couldn't let her down now. He thought of the new Winchester in his store. He could sit on a roof around town and pick off the sheriff as he made his nightly rounds. The town would be rid of an outrage, and society would be better off.

But he had never shot anyone, let alone set out to kill in cold, deliberate fashion. No, he couldn't do it. In a fit of rage, perhaps, but not this way. He hoped that the new man, Spur McCoy, might do the job for him. If Sheriff Johnson threatened to make it public that he was a squaw man, or if he tried to tell Wendy, Nehemiah Hardy swore a silent oath that he would kill the sheriff and be glad that he did!

CHAPTER SEVEN

Spur made it out of Kate Fowler's bedroom and away from the widow's house before the sheriff stormed into the front room. The lawman was hunting his deputy, and Spur could hear him as Spur went down the alley and headed for the hotel.

He'd had a good lunch and then watched the business firms close up. He went to the Red Eye Saloon and lifted a beer. By that time it was nearly eight o'clock and Spur was totaling up his assets on this assignment. He had a rogue sheriff, a sexy widow who might testify for him; Jodi, who was good in bed but not much help on the project, and the newsman Les Van Dyke. The publisher was getting mad enough to blow his top in print and earn himself an early pine box.

Spur didn't think the emporium owner Nehemiah Hardy would be much help. There did seem to be some deep seated anger just below the surface, but McCoy had no way of knowing how to trigger that. He would see Van Dyke later tonight. The fewer people the sheriff saw Spur talking to the better.

The sheriff himself of River Bend county pushed through the bat wing doors and scanned the drinkers. His gaze stopped at Spur and he marched up to him.

"Those don't look like knife selling clothes, mister."

"I'm off work, so I wear what I like. And I talk to whoever I want to." Spur turned his back on the sheriff.

"Turn around, asshole, or get your back sliced open!"

Spur turned suddenly, powering a backhand left fist that slammed against the sheriff's jaw and drove him sideways and to his knees. The lawman shook his head and reached for one of his two pistols.

"Hold it!" Spur barked at him. "Touch that iron and you earn yourself a pine box. You want to stand up nice and easy like and talk like a gentleman, I'll listen. Otherwise take your wise mouth and your convict deputies and get the hell out of here!"

Sheriff Johnson glared at Spur, his hand itching to draw, his brain telling him not to. He got to his feet slowly. Hatred seeped out of every pore in his body. Spur could feel the heat of his anger. With a great deal of control, the sheriff at last could talk.

"What was that crack about convict deputies?"

"Pistol Pete Cody Bovert, for one. He's wanted in at least four states I've been in lately. He has more wanted posters on him than Wes Hardin."

"Wanted? I don't believe it."

"Ask him. He was so stupid he didn't even change his first two names. Pistol Pete—how could anybody be dumb enough not to change that name?"

"I'm looking for him right now. He didn't come to work today. You seen Pistol Pete?"

"Sure, twice, that's why I knew it was him, crescent scar and all. Saw him when I got off the stage and again last night on the street."

"Nobody's seen him today. You seen him, McCoy?"

"Nope, have you?"

"You got a smart mouth, McCoy. One of these days I'll shut it for you, permanently."

"Is that a threat, Sheriff? I understand you and your deputies shot down eleven men and one woman in the past four months."

"Line of duty. They were all low class riff-raff."

"Like the preacher, Fowler? That kind of riff-raff?"

The sheriff quivered with rage. His eyes bulged, his hands hovered over his gun butts again.

"What's the matter, Sheriff? Isn't Pete here to back up your hand anymore?"

The sheriff roared in fury and charged McCoy. The big man waited until the last second, spun aside and slammed his fist down on the sheriff's neck as he careened past. Sheriff Johnson kept right on going, rammed into a bar chair, tipped over a table and rolled on his back.

Spur watched him a moment, then swept a half-filled glass of beer off a table and poured the contents on the sheriff's face. The lawman came up sputtering and swearing. He grabbed one gun but Spur kicked it out of his hand.

"Johnson, you're all through in this town. As of today nobody is going to be afraid of you. Nobody is going to take you seriously. I'd bet you'll be losing some more of your bully boy deputies in the next few days. They just aren't made for honest lawkeeping. Take my advice, Johnson. Pull off that badge right now, grab your money out of the bank and ride just as far and as fast as you can before the good people of this town rise up and shoot you so full of holes they'll use you for a drain gauge."

Spur heard some brief cheers from the thirty odd men in the saloon.

Sheriff Johnson got to his feet slowly.

"You're under arrest, McCoy, for the murder of Pistol Pete, and for assault on a law officer." He slowly drew his second pistol and pointed to two men in the crowd. "You, and you, I'm appointing you special deputies. Move over there and get his gun, and take him to the jail."

One of the men he pointed at shook his head and dove into the crowd. The other one shivered, but moved forward. He made the mistake of getting between Spur and the sheriff. The moment he crossed, Spur pushed the man into the sheriff who was trying to stand. Both tumbled to the floor. Spur sprinted for the door and was through the batwings before the sheriff could find the gun he had dropped. There were roars of laughter inside the saloon, then a shot and the bar mirror showered into hundreds of pieces.

Spur dashed down the street and around the corner. He stormed down the alley to the door where the girls lived and hoped it was not locked. Quickly he pulled the door, it came open and he was inside.

Rebecca stood at the kitchen sink peeling potatoes. She turned, the knife still in her hand, and glared at him.

"Hello, Rebecca. Sorry I had to burst in this way, but the sheriff was chasing me. I'll leave just as soon as I can. Is there another way out of here?"

Her eyes flared angrily for a moment. Then she touched her forehead with her empty hand and when she turned back she was smiling. The knife was in the pan of potatoes.

"Hello, Mr. McCoy. Nice to see you again. Jodi is still taking her bath. I'll tell her you're here."

"No, no, that's all right. I thought you smiled when I asked if there was another way out of here. I didn't necessarily mean a door. Some other way?"

She grinned. "We're not supposed to know it's there. But there is another way. Somebody built a walkway over the top of the gambling hall. I think they cheated that way with the cards. Anyway, it's in here."

In Rebecca's bedroom there was a panel that slid to one side. Beyond it a long corridor, narrow and low, led away into the darkness. Rebecca gave him a candle and a match to light it. He went ahead with the flickering light. Here and there were peek holes into the rooms below. The first part of the corridor led over bedrooms. One was occupied by two people in an age-old wrestling match. Beyond them came the card-rooms—three small ones, then the casino-like main room, with the dance hall girls and small tables for poker and faro.

A cool draft flowed through the corridor and ahead he could see lights. Soon he came to a partition that opened on the second floor balcony leading to the stairway to the third floor. Spur pushed the panel back, stepped out leaving the candle at the end of the corridor. He pushed the panel back in place and ran quickly down the stairs, around two blocks and in to the back door of the newspaper office.

Lights were on. Les Van Dyke wore a paper hat made out of a sheet of newspaper and swore as he worked on the small flat bed press. It was an old model that had to be hand cranked and pressure put on each page to make the impression. He looked up and laughed.

"You don't waste any time making enemies

when you get started. The sheriff was already in here looking for you. He was so mad he was even nice to me. Hear you burned his ears off with some true words over in the saloon."

"Something like that."

"Just in time. Some cowboy riding the grub line found your buddy Pistol Pete in the Greybull about ten miles downstream. Figured he was a lawman by his tin badge, so he carted the bloated corpse back up here. Your friend the sheriff has really got a wild hair up his ass."

"So now we take the kid gloves off and the real fight begins. What can you help me get done?"

"What needs doing?"

"Who else know anything about the Fowler shooting? I may have one circumstantial witness, but I need somebody who actually saw the man gunned down. Got any names?"

"None alive. Word was that Pete pulled the trigger on orders from on up the line, Johnson."

"But did anyone *see* Pete pull the trigger?"

"Not that I've heard of. You talk to the widow?"

"Yes. But I'd hate to put her on the witness stand."

"Don't worry about that. She's fucked half the grown men and boys in town. No local jury would believe anything she said. She thinks with her crotch."

"Maybe now that there's some opposition, our friend the sheriff will do something stupid that we can pin on him," Spur said. "Do we have an honest district attorney in this county?"

"Yep, but his assistant is bought and paid for by the sheriff so he knows everything that happens."

"Who is the assistant?"

"Kid by the name of Yale Crowningshield. He's reading for the law and thinks he's hot piss."

"I'll have to have a talk with the lad."

"Somebody left a message for you today. I don't know why or who but it was on the door when I got back from lunch." Les handed the envelope to Spur who tore it open. Inside was a small sheet of paper with printing on it. It read:

I have something valuable for you. It is vital that you get it today. Come to livery stable in midnight.

There was no signature.

Spur showed it to Les, who read it and shrugged. "I always ignore anonymous messages. The person who wrote this printed it so it wouldn't point to any kind of type of person, young, old, literate, etc. Could be almost anyone."

"But probably not the sheriff," Spur said. "He's the only one I really won't go out of my way to see. The letter said something valuable. That could be a witness or something to tie up the sheriff."

"How many people know that's what you're looking for?"

"Not many, true." Spur helped Les rip open a new package of paper. "Well, I'll have to decide whether to go or not. At least I have a couple of hours. You going to work all night?"

"Only until I get this week's issue printed."

"Want some help? I can fold and stuff."

Les looked at him. "Sounds like you've been around a newspaper plant before."

"Now and then. Which ones are dry? Show me what to insert and then fold. Let's get this organized!"

Two hours later the paper was done, folded and ready to deliver to the four places in town in the morning. Spur left by the back way and went into the livery stable by the corral gate. He climbed to the loft without a sound and sat by the hay feed door near the front where they put down hay for the stock. He could see the front door and the small office to one side. There was a light on low, and he could see a wrangler sleeping in a bunk. Who had said he would meet Spur here at midnight? The agent settled down. He would give the guy a half hour, then he was going to go to sleep in the hay.

CHAPTER EIGHT

Spur McCoy waited fifteen minutes, growing more impatient all the time. He had moved once to the other side of the hay feed hole, then settled down.

Without warning someone jumped into the hay beside him. He pawed for his gun as he turned hoping he wasn't too late. He came up with the six-gun and stared, almost nose to nose with the impish grin of Violet, the dark-haired, black-eyed, seventeen-year-old who had darted into his room at the hotel that first night he was in town.

She laughed softly when she saw his weapon.

"I promise I won't hurt you, Spur. You can put away that gun."

McCoy relaxed. "The little girl with the mole on her breast. I remember you."

"You forgot to say I have big tits and that I want you to make love to me." She shrugged out of her blouse, and Spur couldn't help but look at her full breasts.

"Come on, kiss me or something so I won't feel foolish. Here you've got me in the hay and my blouse is off. You're the one who is supposed to know what to do."

Spur sighed, bent and kissed her pouting lips and changed her frown to a glorious smile.

"Oh, yes! That was heaven! I knew you would steal my cherry. I just knew it! Let's move back from here a ways so we don't get all excited and fall through."

Spur cupped one of her breasts in his hand. "Violet, I'm not going to make love to you."

"Oh shit. Why the fuck not?"

"Don't swear and talk dirty, it isn't ladylike."

"I don't want to be a lady!" She hissed at him, her voice rising. "I just want to know what it feels like to be caressed and seduced and fucked by a real man like you!"

"You have lots of time for that, the rest of your life. That comes after you get a husband. That's your first big task."

"Oh, *that*. I can get married anytime I want to. Been asked four times already. Two of them were older men. One was a foreman at the mines!"

"Good, pick out one and get married before you

make a mistake like this."

She touched his crotch and he moved her hand. "Come on Spur, give me a chance. You're touching me. Let me mess around a little."

He was tempted. She was delicious, new and unused, unspoiled, trainable. He bent and kissed her breasts, then chewed lightly on both nipples.

Violet tensed, then she went rigid and fell on top of him, her body quivering with a climax. He held her so they wouldn't fall through the hole and she moaned softly as the tremors shot through her sleek young body again and again. His hand found her breasts and he massaged them tenderly until she gave a soft little cry and went limp against him.

A minute later she lifted her head, then moved his hand back to her breasts and sighed.

"Spur, that was glorious! Absolutely fantastic. Now let me get my skirt off and you can poke my little pussy."

"No." He looked at her in the dimness of the hayloft. "Violet, did you leave that note for me at the newspaper office?"

"Yes, and you came."

"I didn't know who it was. I have other important things I have to do."

"I only want another half hour so you can make love to me."

"NO. Now put back on your blouse."

"You don't like me. You think I'm ugly."

"You're ugly, yes, if that's what it takes to get rid of you. I'm going out the back door. If you really want to become a tramp, a prostitute, a

87

slut, you'll find lots of men to help you. But I don't think you want that. I've given you a little thrill. Now go home and finish growing up. Then send me a note in about three years.''

Spur moved away from her, walking through the packed down hay to the back door where he went down a ladder, through the corral and over the fence.

Violet again. He had forgotten how sweet and delicious a seventeen-year-old girl could be. When he had been young he'd never properly appreciated them. He shook his head. That was one type in which he could not afford to become interested. Furious fathers had a way of shooting first and charging a man with rape second—if the victim lived.

Spur knew that he could not go back to either of the hotels for a night's sleep. Instead he tried the alley door where the girls lived. It was locked. Too late to wake them. He went to the stairway, climbed to the second storey and found the panel in front. He slid it back far enough to enter and closed it. The candle was where he had left it. Spur lit it with a stinker match and soon slid the panel to one side in Rebecca's room.

She had left a lamp burning low. Rebecca slept soundly, one arm thrown out and her nightgown in a pile on the floor. She moved and her breasts showed above the sheet. He moved on quietly, went out her door toward the other bedroom. He could see a light burning under the door. Spur blew out the candle and edged the panel open.

Jodi sat up in bed reading a book. She glanced

up expectantly as she heard the door open.

"Spur?" she asked. Her green eyes probed the darkness around the door.

"Yes. I need a place to sleep tonight. The sheriff has the hotels covered."

"I have a warm bed for you," Jodi said. She pulled a thin nightgown over her head and sat there watching him, her big breasts swaying gently from her body motion.

"Don't undress," she said. "Come here, with your boots on and your pants, everything. I want you just the way you are. Your clothes will feel rough on me."

Jodi kicked off the sheet and lifted her spread legs high in the air.

"I've been sitting here thinking about you. I've had about two hours of getting warmed up Please get up here and slam it right into me!"

Spur did. He realized he had been more excited by the nubile teenager than he wanted to admit. She had been damn tempting, but Jodi was much more practical. They plunged together into a crashing, shouting, exhausting climax and then lay side by side talking. Spur undressed.

"I hear you knocked down our sheriff today, and then tongue-lashed him to a fare-thee-well. Our Sheriff Johnson does not like that. He may have some misgivings about you now."

Spur laughed. "Afraid you're right. Sometimes my mouth gets me in trouble."

"There's some talk around town that you were the one who shot Deputy Pistol Pete."

"Just speculation. They want to blame it on me

so nobody else in town will be suspect."

"Are you any closer to tying the sheriff to the Rev. Fowler's shooting?"

"Is the word around town that I'm working on that, too?"

"I hear most everything at the Emporium. I know for certain that my boss, Mr. Hardy, would like to see the sheriff jailed and convicted."

"The more people who feel that way, the quicker we'll get the job done."

"Another fun playtime?" she asked.

"No, let's talk."

"Fine. It's nice, you know? Nice just lying here beside you and feeling all warm and soft inside. Knowing that you'll be there in the morning when I wake up. Kind of great. Maybe that's what it's like to be married."

"Probably. I wouldn't know."

"Now, don't get skitterish. I wasn't hinting."

"How is Rebecca?"

"Fine, usually. Once in a while she gets frightened. You know she carried knives in her skirts. She's got a knife sewn in a pocket in the folds of each one. Probably just a fear of men. One of these days maybe . . ." Jodi stopped and shook her head. "No, I probably shouldn't mess with that idea at all."

"What idea?"

She turned to him, green eyes worried, unsure. "You know she was molested when she was young, and raped, and then she killed our father. It left scars and troubles her deeply. But I was wondering, maybe . . . No, forget it."

90

"What are you suggesting?"

"Maybe if someone could show her that sex between a man and woman was natural, not terrible, she would get over her terror of men."

"Possibly. I had a doctor friend in Washington who specialized in crazy people. He said some of them could regain their sanity, but it would take a long time, a lot of work and care. Might be the same with Rebecca."

"Probably. I shouldn't have talked about it. As long as she doesn't get in trouble, or hurt anyone, I guess we can go on this way."

"Wasn't there something yesterday about a man being killed with a knife back here in the alley?"

"I heard that. But men get in knife fights all the time. Somebody is bound to get hurt."

"Yeah, you're right." He kissed her gently, then said goodnight and was asleep quickly.

Jodi thought about the dead man in the alley. No, it couldn't be. Rebecca never went out of their rooms unless Jodi went with her.

But Jodi thought about it until she went to sleep. There was a chance that Rebecca had been in the alley that night, but there was no way to find out for sure. Jodi pondered it again as she dropped off to sleep, one hand on Spur McCoy's shoulder.

CHAPTER NINE

Rebecca sat across the table from Spur and Jodi, watching them as they ate.

"You two going to get married?" Rebecca asked. "You been sleeping together, so I wondered."

"No, we're not getting married, Rebecca," Jodi said before Spur could react. "Although I wouldn't mind at all. You see, good friends sometimes do that, sleep together, even though they are not getting married. Rebecca, making love is the most wonderful thing anyone can experience. It's beautiful, tender, marvelous. You will find out about that someday."

For a moment Rebecca's eyes burned with a strange, savage glow, then she shrugged.

"Maybe. I don't much like men."

"That will change, Rebecca," Spur said. "One of these days you'll meet a fine young man and learn to like him a lot."

"Not if he tries to touch me!" Her eyes blazed again.

"Touching isn't that bad, Rebecca," Spur said. "Here, touch my hand. You touch me."

"That's different." She reached out and touched his hand, then his arm. When he started to hold her hand she jerked it back.

"No!"

"It may take a while," Jodi sighed. "Now, what are we going to do today, Becky? Is that new chair cover done yet, the cross-stitch you were working on?"

Rebecca recovered at once. "No, not yet. I'll get busy on it today."

Spur finished his breakfast of eggs and bacon and reached for his hat.

"Going to talk to the district attorney this morning. See what kind of law enforcement you have in this county. I don't expect any results, but I could get lucky. Does the courthouse open at eight?"

"Usually. It's not a big courthouse. In fact it's two rooms in the Bayless building just down from the hotel. This isn't a rich county."

"I noticed. Can I walk you to work?"

She said he could, and a few minutes later they

paused in front of the store. She touched his shoulder.

"You be careful. Don't do anything to give the sheriff a clean shot at you, legally or with his bully boys. I want you back in my bed tonight."

"You're trying to wear me out."

"I'd love to try." She smiled and went into the Emporium general store.

Spur walked another block to the Bayless building and went through the door marked "River Bend County Offices."

It *was* a poor county. From what Spur could see there were only four employees for the county, besides the sheriff, and they were all on the premises.

A small gray-haired lady with spectacles looked up from a big ledger as he stepped to the elbow high counter that ran across the twenty-foot wide room.

"I'd like to see the district attorney," Spur said.

"Yes sir. He'll be right here." She went to one of two other desks in the room and a moment later a man in a black suit and string tie came to the counter.

"Clyde Oberholtzer. How can I help you?"

"Where can we talk in private?"

The man's glance darted toward Spur. "Private?"

"Extremely private."

"Over by the window. We don't have separate offices yet. It's in the new building plans."

They sat by the window in straight backed

chairs and the man watched Spur expectantly.

"You're the new man in town who has been arguing with our sheriff?"

"Yes, and you're the district attorney?"

"Right."

"Good. I want to swear out a citizen's complaint against the sheriff and his three deputies, charging them with murder, with conspiracy to murder, with malfeasance in office, and grand theft. I want them arrested and no bail set due to the extreme seriousness of the cases and the fact that they would then have the power to bring illegal duress against the complainant masquerading it as their legal law enforcement duty. I think you'll find this action justified and with precedent."

Oberholtzer sat back, surprised. "Those are serious charges. Before I swore out a complaint, I would need some evidence, some legal testimony that would stand up in court."

"I have such evidence. A sworn statement by a witness who heard Sheriff Johnson order one of his deputies, Pete Bovert, to kill the Rev. Mr. Fowler."

"Yes, that is evidence, I must say," he smiled. "The people of the county would cheer roundly if this could work. But, I don't see how I can do it. Who would be our law enforcement?"

"You have the legal right to appoint an acting sheriff and allow him to deputize as many men as he needs."

"If only it would work! You don't know how the honest people in this county have been praying for something like this. But what if it doesn't hold? What if a judge throws it out of court?"

"Then we would have a start. We could hold a recall election and throw the sheriff out of office. With no power, he would cause a little hell here and then move on."

"Probably, but only after killing you and me. Do you want to risk that?"

"Yes. Where are the papers so I can fill them out and get this started?"

It was almost two hours later before Spur had the papers completed, his complaint written out in triplicate and filed with the district attorney. He had read them as Spur was writing, nodding and exclaiming. When Spur finished and he read the last page, Oberholtzer nodded.

"It could work, and it could stick. We're going to need more evidence for a jury, but this should get it started. Once we get him in jail, I think more people will come forward with evidence."

"Now, one more thing. I'm told Yale Crowning-shield is on the sheriff's payroll. Can you keep these charges from him until you arrest the sheriff?"

"Yale is being bribed by the sheriff? That's another charge if we can prove it. Something like this is hard to keep quiet in a small town. I'll try."

Spur left the courthouse and walked to a side street. He had just turned the corner leading to the alley where they girls lived when he heard a six-gun cock behind him.

"Hold it right here, asshole!"

Before he turned around, Spur knew it was the sheriff. He made sure his hands were not moving and nowhere near his weapon. He turned slowly.

"Good morning, Johnson. From what I hear around town you've got a death wish."

"A what?" Johnson said, not understanding. It took the initiative away from him.

"You keep doing all these wild, dangerous things just hoping that one of them will kill you. A death wish. You're too yellow to shoot yourself so you keep hoping somebody else will."

The sheriff waved his gun at Spur. "If anybody dies around here, it's gonna be you. I'm arresting you for the murder of Pistol Pete. He told one of my deputies the night before he vanished that he was dead certain he knew you from somewhere before. Dead certain, he said. I think you killed him."

"I takes proof to arrest somebody. Where's yours?"

"I'll get it, somehow." He frowned. "Or maybe I should just save the county the cost of the trial."

"You've been doing that a lot lately."

"So what does one more hurt?"

"Not a thing," Spur said. "Except for those six people behind you watching. Be hard to convince them that it was a case of self defense, or my resisting arrest or trying to escape."

He looked over his shoulder for just a second. That was all Spur needed. He drew his six-gun as he dove for the ground and brought the weapon up firing a shot into the lawman's gun hand shoulder before he could get off a shot. There were people behind them. Nehemiah Hardy, Jodi, and three others Spur didn't know.

The sheriff dropped his weapon, roared with pain and anger and started to draw his second six-gun with his left hand.

"Touch it, Sheriff, and you're a dead man. Would save the county a trial, come to think of it."

Johnson started twice to take the gun out of the holster, but each time he stopped. Then he grabbed his shoulder with his left hand and glared at Spur.

"Gunning a peace officer. I got you good now, McCoy."

"Not so, ex-Sheriff. I'm placing you under citizen's arrest for attempted murder and extortion. My own murder. Just stand steady and I'll relieve you of that weapon."

Spur took the Colt from its leather, picked up the other one from the ground and shoved both inside his belt. Then he marched Johnson up the street.

"First we go see the doctor to get you patched up. Then you go into one of your own jail cells."

Sheriff Johnson's face was so red Spur thought he was going to explode. Blood seeped down his shirt sleeve. His fringed leather vest had spots of blood on it. His eyes went wild with hatred and fury.

"You'll not get half way to the jail, bastard! My men will cut you down like the asshole you are!" They walked to Main Street and Johnson looked around frantically. At last he saw one of his men.

"Take him, Winslow! Blow him into hell!"

Spur saw the man lift his six-gun. In the split second left him, Spur jumped behind Johnson, using him as a shield.

"Go ahead, Winslow," Spur called. "Put a couple of bullets right through the sheriff. Did Johnson tell you that he's under arrest for attempted murder, for murder, for conspiracy, and about a dozen other charges?"

Spur wasn't paying enough attention to the sheriff. He swung his good left hand, slapping Spur's weapon out of his hand and powering the agent away from his protection. Two shots thundered from forty feet away. Spur hit the ground rolling, came on his feet running and got behind a buckboard at the boardwalk. He dodged again, into a store, and bolted through to the back door where he got out and into the alley.

A minute later he banged on the door where Rebecca let him inside. He was panting, he was dirt smeared and dusty.

Rebecca looked different. She had on a tight dress that made her good breasts surge forward. A thin line of cleavage showed at the low neckline. She smiled a strange smile, and he nodded.

"Somebody chasing me again. Don't tell anyone I was here."

He had to go past her. As he did to get to her bedroom door, he bent and kissed her lips gently, then ran on. He failed to see an expression of anger on her face that quickly changed to delight.

She lifted her fingers to touch her lips, and stared after him.

Spur was through the hidden panel and into the passageway. He didn't bother with a candle this time, simply moving quietly and quickly toward the front of the building. He had tied it this time. He couldn't stay in town, at least not anywhere he could be seen. The sheriff would be after him now with every weapon and every man he had. He had to know he was fighting for his life.

When Spur came to the front of the passageway, he looked through a crack at the balcony and the street. A good place to bide his time. Twice in the next half hour he saw a deputy with a badge pinned on his vest work slowly up the street, looking at everyone, checking in each store along the way. The deputy even came up the stairs and looked into the second storey building. Spur could have reached out and touched him.

When the deputy left, Spur made his decision. It was time he checked out the last element in this equation, the rancher, Hans Klanhouser. His place was north of town and just across the Greybull River. He should be able to find it. He would wait there in the passageway until dark, then he would get down to the livery, rent a horse and saddle and strike out for the ranch. Somebody said it was ten miles out of town. He would be there in a couple of hours.

Then Spur heard movement behind him in the passage. He drew his revolver and cocked the hammer muffling the sound. Whoever was coming would get a hot lead reception.

CHAPTER TEN

Spur McCoy realized he was silhouetted against the light coming in from the secret opening behind him. He moved cautiously toward the sounds for ten feet then stopped. He held his breath and listened. Yes, the sounds were still coming, someone moving slowly. There was no lighted candle.

He waited another three or four minutes and he could hear the other person breathing.

"Ouch! Oh, dear!"

Spur heard the words and the woman's voice. A woman? Jodi or Rebecca? It could be no one else.

He let the hammer down soundlessly on his weapon, but still held it. Someone might be forcing her to come, to show him the passage.

Two minutes more and he could see a form ahead of him in the blackness. One form. He caught the flash of the same dress. It was Rebecca.

"Rebecca?" Spur whispered.

There was silence for a while. Her movement stopped.

"Yes. Spur?"

"Right, what are you doing in here?"

"I . . . I just wanted to see what was at the other end. I've never been through it."

He told her where it came out. They both walked hunched over toward the opening. He showed her the street and she giggled.

"Strange, it seemed so far."

"I have to stay here until it's dark outside. The sheriff wants to shoot me."

"Oh, no!" she said surprising him with her reaction. "He can't do that. I'll tell him not to."

"Right now he's real mad at me. He wouldn't listen to you."

He saw now that the dress seemed even tighter. One of the buttons on the bodice had come undone, letting more of her breasts show.

Spur sat down in the narrow passage. "I have to stay until dark so I'm going to be comfortable. Do you want to wait with me?"

"Oh yes. That would be nice."

She sat beside him, so close their thighs touched.

"How long have you been here in Elk Creek?" he asked.

"Long, two or three years." She turned toward him. "Spur, would you touch me?" Her face took on a frown and he saw just a glint of the anger building in her eyes, then it faded. "I want . . . I want to be able to stand it when you touch me."

"Yes. Of course." He put his hand over hers where it lay on her leg. For a moment she tensed, then she took a deep breath and let it out slowly.

"I like the feeling. Yes, I like it. Touch my shoulder."

He did and she took another breath.

"Would you . . . would you put your arm around my shoulders?"

Spur did, watching her reaction. This time the anger surged stronger in her face, but she beat it down with a new found strength.

"Yes! Yes!" She turned her face toward him, which was close now, and he saw her beaming in relief and joy. "Yes, I can do it! I can let a man touch me!" For just a moment she relaxed and leaned against him, then sat up straighter.

"Spur, I appreciate this. I really do. I . . . I have been having some bad days lately. It all seems so useless. I . . . I had some terrible experiences when I was younger."

"Don't think about them, just think about now," Spur said. "About how it feels good when I hug you. It's going to take some time. But you have made a good start."

She leaned against him and shivered, then turned her face toward his.

105

"One more thing. Would you . . . would you kiss me the way you did in my room?"

He bent and brushed her lips with his, then came away. Her eyes were closed, and she sighed, then smiled. He did the same thing again, then when her hand reached out and touched him, he kissed her again, firmly on her mouth, and pulled away.

She sat there with her eyes closed, a smile on her face.

"That felt so good, Spur. It was wonderful. Now, just one more touch, then I have to leave." She picked up his hand and brought it to her breasts. They felt hot to his touch where they surged halfway out of her dress. She kept her hand on top of his and pressed it firmly on her bosom. She held it there for a full minute, then pulled his hand away, and smiled softly.

"Thank you, Spur. Thanks a lot!" She leaned in, kissed his lips quickly and stood. She bent over and walked down the narrow passageway. She never looked back.

Spur sat there a moment smiling after her. She just might make it into the human race yet. He worked quietly back to the passage opening and watched through the cracks. It wouldn't be dark for a long time.

Spur lay down on the bare boards and went to sleep. He would need the rest before this was over.

He woke up just before midnight, surprised that he had slept so long. No matter. He slipped out the opening, closed it and headed for the closest alley and to the livery stable.

Spur spent the two hours before dawn taking a nap less than half a mile from the buildings of the Circle K ranch. He had ridden here easily from town and waited for the sun to come up. When he heard the breakfast bell ring at the big mess hall, he rode in.

A rifle toting guard picked him up a quarter of a mile out and talked to him. Just a precaution, the guard said and told Spur to go on in and have breakfast.

He tied his horse to a hitching rail in front of the building and opened the door. Heads turned. An older man stood up and watched him.

"Mr. Klanhouser?" Spur asked.

The man nodded. "Sit down and eat, then we'll talk. I ain't hiring but a man is always welcome to breakfast."

Spur had forgotten about chuck wagon cooking. There were ten men at the long plank table, and a dozen trays filled with fried eggs, flapjacks, pitchers of coffee, bacon and sausage, stacks of toast, pitchers of milk and a big bowl of applesauce.

He was hungry and ate all he wanted, then took his cup of coffee and sat across from the ranch owner.

"Not looking for work," Spur said. "But I would like to talk to you for a few minutes."

Klanhouser nodded. He was a thickset man, with black hair that needed cutting, heavy eyebrows that shadowed gray eyes, and a nose that dominated his face. He wore a full beard and

107

moustache.

"Got to ride up north about three miles to check out two dead steers. Welcome to ride along."

It took Spur two miles of easy riding to tell the ranch owner exactly why he was in Elk Creek and what he hoped to get done here.

"Do you have any hard evidence that I can use against the sheriff? It has to be proof that will stand up in court and convince a jury."

Hans Klanhouser stopped his bay and took off his low-crowned hat, wiped sweat off his forehead with his arm and nodded.

"Might have. The sheriff gunned down one of my riders in town about two months ago. Claimed he was wild drunk and shooting up the saloon. Said Jason drew down on the sheriff and he had to fire to save his own life."

"Any of your men witness the shooting?"

"Saw the whole thing. Jason won two hundred dollars off the sheriff at a poker game in the Long Trail Saloon. Two of my riders was in the same game. Sheriff arrested Jason on the spot and took him out the front door. By the time my other men got out there the sheriff had out his gun and Jason was trying to get his. He wasn't no shooter. Jason almost got himself killed cause he tried to shoot a rattler one day. Missed it five times from three feet.

"Anyways, the sheriff shot him twice from about ten feet. Late at night, nobody else on the street. Jason never got his iron out of leather."

"Now we're getting something solid," Spur

said. "I want the dead man's name, and the exact date when this happened. Are the riders still with you who saw all this?"

"Yep. One of them is my son. I'll give you the names. Now let's see what killed them steers. I just lost another eighty dollars. Steer worth forty dollars on the hoof down at the rail yards in Rawlins."

"The sheriff ever get out this way?"

"Never has. I talked to him one day in town. He told me what went on at the Circle K was my problem. The town situation was all his, and I was to keep my nose out of it. I don't let the men go in more than once a month. I don't want any more of them getting killed."

Spur spent the rest of the day there. He wrote down everything he could find out about the killing of Jason Roberts. He talked with both the witnesses, and took down the exact words they used in describing the card game, the loss, then the arrest and subsequent unprovoked killing.

Any district attorney would drool over an open and shut case like this one. But the sheriff being the killer made it a tough case to prosecute.

Spur stayed over in the bunk house that night and headed back for Elk Creek just after breakfast. He would be in town about ten, and would try to get to the courthouse without the sheriff spotting him.

But Spur didn't make it to town. He had just crossed the river at the ford a half mile out of town when somebody with a rifle opened up on him. The first round missed him but he could hear

109

the whistle of the bullet. He dove off the back of his mount and the next round caught the mare in the head, knocking her down. She screamed for two minutes before Spur put a mercy round into her head, ending her misery.

He crawled away from the dead mare and the rifleman fired again. Spur sprinted ten yards to a pile of boulders and slid behind them as a round whined off the rocks. He crawled the next ten yards to the side of the river and rolled over into the twenty foot deep gully the Spring rains had gouged. Now the river was low allowing plenty of room along the dry bank.

Spur charged forward toward the spot he figured the rounds had come from. He had to get close to do any good with his six-gun. Somehow he figured the bushwhacker would sit in place, knowing Spur had no long gun. He would wait for a chance at Spur as he ran for town aross the flat lands.

The agent crawled up the bank to check his progress. The clump of cottonwoods was still fifty yards from him. He watched but could see no motion at the fringe of the green leaves. Another three minute run and he spotted the cottonwood tops. He went past them, when he came up to the lip of the bank and looked over.

He saw through the trees, and a pair of blue pants and tan shirt where the sniper lay behind a long fallen log.

Spur wished he had brought along a rifle. A Spencer would come in handy. Without it he was too far away to trust the six-gun. It was a new one to him. He bought it from the stable hand when he rented the horse. So he would have to be closer.

Spur worked up the side of the wash, crawled behind some brush and stood. The sniper was moving around. He peered over the log, then stood behind a tree, but was still looking to the front. McCoy needed another twenty feet to get in practical range.

There was no cover between him and the sniper. Spur stepped from the last cottonwood tree and walked quietly forward. He was still sixty feet away. He moved cautiously, without breaking a twig.

Fifty feet.

The man turned. Spur screamed and charged straight ahead, his weapon up and held with both hands as he aimed as he ran.

Forty feet.

The sniper's surprise cost him a second's hesitation, and that was what killed him. By the time he got the long gun swung around and up to aim, Spur was thirty feet from him and the Colt in his hand barked four times.

Three of the big slugs caught the sniper in the chest and bowled him over backwards. Two of the rounds roared through the victim's heart dumping him into the quiet blackness of never ending death.

Spur walked up and looked down at the man's face. He had not seen the bushwhacker around town. A new hire perhaps.

The agent went through the man's pockets. He

found four dollars in cash, a cheap watch and a folded piece of paper. Spur unfolded it and found a good description of himself, as well as the exact color of his horse and saddle type that he had rented.

The sheriff was covering all bases. The Secret Service agent checked the rifle, a Spencer seven shot repeater. The kind he liked. He found half a dozen rounds in the sniper's pockets, then looked for his horse. Seemed like a fair trade, one chance to bushwhack him for his rifle and horse. The six-gun the man carried was a relic, a .32. Spur would rather throw rocks at someone than try to hit them with the old .32.

He found the horse in the next smattering of trees upstream two hundred yards. Spur changed his mind about the mount when he saw it. She was almost as worn out as the six-gun. The saddle was a duplicate of his own. Evidently both horse and saddle had been rented from the livery in Elk Creek. He unsaddled the animal, took off the halter and whacked her on the rump. Let her have a year of freedom before she died of old age. She might join some wandering herd of wild horses.

Spur walked toward town. He circled off the trail and came in behind some houses not far from the livery.

He shook his head in sudden memory and realization as he walked along. His college friends would laugh at him if they could see him today. He had not started out as a cowboy. He was born and grew up in New York City where his father was a big time retailer and importer. Spur graduated from Harvard in the class of 1858 and went into business with his father for two years. Then the war began and he enlisted as a second lieutenant in the infantry. He advanced to a captain's rank. After two years in the army he went to Washington, D.C. to serve as an aide to Senator Arthur B. Walton, a long-time family friend.

In 1865, soon after the act was passed, Charles Spur McCoy was appointed one of the first twelve U.S. Secret Service Agents. Since the Secret Service was the only federal law enforcement agency at that time, it handled a wide range of problems. Most of these jobs were far removed from the group's original task of preventing currency counterfeiting.

Spur served six months in the Washington office, then was transferred to head the base in St. Louis and handled all cases west of the Mississippi. He had been chosen from ten applicants because he was the only one who could ride a horse well, and because he had won the service marksmanship contest. His boss, William Wood, figured Spur would need both skills in the wild west.

And he had.

As he came into town he pulled his hat down low over his face and watched for the sheriff or any of his deputies.

He came in the back door of the livery and grabbed the same stable man he had rented his horse from.

"Pardner, did the sheriff talk to you last night after I rented that horse? You lie about it and I'll pound the truth out of you."

The man spit a stream of tobaco juice into the dust, and nodded.

"Sure he did. You didn't tell me nothing about secrets. So I described you and the horse."

"You almost got me killed. Somebody tried to bushwhack me outside of town. Instead he killed your horse. You can bill the sheriff for the nag and pick up the saddle a half mile out anytime you want to. Now I am asking you to keep a secret. I'm trying to get rid of this sheriff and do it all legal. You want to help me, you just don't tell him or his deputies that I got back in one chunk. You understand?"

"Yes sir. I don't like our sheriff either."

Spur McCoy changed his mind, paid for the dead horse, shouldered the Spencer and looked out the livery door into the street. Now all he had to do was figure out how to stay alive until he could check with the district attorney, and see if he could arrest the sheriff.

CHAPTER ELEVEN

Sheriff Tyler Johnson paused beside a cell in his jail and grinned.

"What's the matter, old timer? Can't you hold your booze no more? We rolled you out of a saloon last night. You sober now?"

"Yeah, Sheriff. Cold, stone sober."

"Good. You want out of jail?"

"Christ yes!"

"Good, I'll tell you what I want you to do. I don't have me no 'representative' in that swill-bag saloon you was in. You keep your eyes and ears open in there and tell me what's going on, and you get out of jail without paying twenty dollars bail."

"Twenty dollars? Hell, Sheriff, you know I ain't had that kind of money in years. Be glad to tell you what I hear."

The sheriff unlocked the jail and gave the man his hat and jacket.

"I'll be in touch with you, old timer, every day."

The sheriff watched him out the door. Things were moving along better. For a while he was jittery, with that new man in town raising hell. But he wouldn't bother him any more, not with a .52 caliber slug in his chest. The district attorney said something about some charges had been filed against the sheriff and Johnson knocked the bastard down and tromped him. He wouldn't be saying anything for a week at least until he healed.

Yeah, and now for some fun. He'd been six months finding out what he needed to know about Nehemiah Hardy. But now he had the information he needed. It was going to be sweet revenge to cut that big shot down to size. And to bring that Wendy Hardy off her high horse. Shit! This was going to be a bucket of belly laughs!

This was the morning that Wendy worked at the store, helping out with the books. Damn! Sheriff Tyler Johnson scratched his balls as he stood there, then rubbed the growing bulge behind his fly. Goddamn, he better get on over there.

When the sheriff came in the front door of the

emporium, Jodi saw him and moved behind a display of crockery tubs. She didn't want to speak to him if she didn't have to. He always tried to undress her with his eyes. Once he had asked her out to dinner, but she turned him down politely.

He went directly to the office and closed the door. A moment later Hardy came out looking pale. He searched for Jodi and found her.

"Can you hold down the place for a while? Something has come up that I have to take care of in the office."

"Sure, just so nobody wants ten rolls of barbed wire."

He nodded but she knew he didn't hear her. He went back into the office. All he could think of was what the sheriff wanted to talk about. They never had any business. He did order ammunition for the county, but that went through the court-house. Hardy sat in his chair behind the small desk with Wendy on the other side. Sheriff Johnson stood near the door. He was pleased to see there was no window in the door. They had a private place.

"Glad you could talk so quick, Hardy. You may not know about it but we've been having a lot of break-ins and robberies lately. That's why we're starting a new service for merchants. We have a special policing service we offer for you. For a hundred dollars a month we'll check your doors and windows twice a night just to make sure nobody is robbing your place.

"Yeah, I know, it seems like a lot of money. But

117

think how much it would cost to replace your front windows if a smash and run criminal came and stole a wagon load of goods."

"That's ridiculous!" Wendy Hardy said. "Our taxes pay for our police protection, and that's you and your men. What you're suggesting is a tribute, a forced contribution, the crudest form of graft and corruption. I'm going right this minute to the county courthouse and tell everyone what you're trying to do."

Hardy stood up and motioned for his wife to sit down. He turned and faced the larger man. "Sheriff, I've heard of this kind of highway robbery in other places. I never thought we would be faced with a payoff like this here. Maybe I misunderstood what you said."

"Hardy, you got it all straight. A hundred U.S. dollars a month or we can't guarantee your safety, or the safety of your store."

"I won't call you Sheriff again, Johnson. You're an insult to the badge and the office. You're nothing but a tin horn hoodlum, an outlaw masquerading behind a badge."

For a big man Johnson moved fast. He hit Hardy with his right fist on the cheek, tearing a flap of skin free. His left hand slammed into Hardy's nose smashing it so the blood ran freely. He slumped back into his chair. Wendy rushed around the desk and put her handkerchief over his nose to stop the blood.

"Lesson one, Hardy. This is my county. Whatever I say here goes. Nobody is going to stand up to me. Not with you and that sneaky newspaper out of the way. And this is just the start, Hardy. You are a special case. I know your family has money in the east, and you have a lot back there too in two separate bank accounts. Didn't you know it's against the law to take money out of the county?

"Your fine is five thousand dollars. Payable this afternoon in cash. If Otto doesn't have it, you tell him to get it as soon as he can, paper or gold, don't matter."

"I won't give you a copper!" Hardy shouted.

"Oh, I think you will. Maybe you want me to tell your wife about that friend you have outside town."

Hardy looked up quickly. "I have friends all around in the mines and the ranches."

"Yeah, especially one ranch. So I'll tell her. Wendy, did you know you're living with a squaw man? True. He met the little Sioux about sixteen years ago, before he met you. They have two little breed bastards out at that ranch he owns. She's his live-in squaw, you're wife number two."

Johnson looked up just in time to see Hardy come at him with a hunting knife. Johnson knocked it out of his hand, slammed him to the floor with a roundhouse right fist and picked up the knife.

Wendy had slumped in the chair shaking her head. Hardy had not denied his squaw! That was what shocked her the most. She had known about the ranch, and that there were a few Indians there, but there had been no hint, no suggestion . . . Or had there? His frequent trips out there.

119

The goods he took out from the store. Yes, fabrics, clothes. She turned her head. Tears seeped from her eyes. How could he!

Johnson stood before them. "So now she knows. But, of course, we're going to have to keep this our little secret. If anyone in town heard about it . . ."

"You wouldn't!" Hardy said from where he sat on the floor. "If that got out it would ruin me. Nobody would buy a thing from me. I'd be bankrupt within a month."

"True, Hardy. Absolutely true. That's why the three of us are going to be very good friends. Wendy, stand up and come here."

There was a ring of authority in his voice. She looked at her husband, but he had hung his head. She stiffened. At least she could show some backbone. She stood in front of him and without warning flashed out her right hand, fingers bent into claws as she raked her nails down his cheek digging four deep furrows there four inches long. Blood oozed from the marks, and one drop dripped to the floor. He caught her hand.

"That was not a smart thing to do, Wendy." He forced her to kneel in front of him. "Wendy, I've got this bad itch. I want you to scratch it for me, gently now." He took her wrist and moved her hand to his crotch.

"Scratch it for me."

She burst into tears. He held her hand on his genitals.

"Now a few tears ain't gonna help. Need that itch scratched."

She wiped the wetness away from her other hand. "You're crude and evil and terrible!"

"That sure ain't taking care of my itch."

She sighed. "I scratch the itch and then you'll go away and leave us alone?"

"Course! I'm a man of my word."

She looked up at him, then slowly her fingers rubbed the bulge she found there. He chuckled.

"Yeah, now that is good. Lower down."

Her fingers curved around the bulge of his scrotum.

"Say, I think you've got the idea." He opened the buttons of his fly and she pulled her hand back. He caught it and when he put it back to his crotch his pants were open and his penis and scrotum both hung in front of her, his long tool half erect.

"You are good, Wendy. Look, Hardy don't mind. Go ahead and help junior down there get all hard. You can do that."

"You promised just some scratching then you would go."

"Shit, I lied, Wendy. I do that a lot. Get me hard, any fucking way you can!"

Hardy screamed and got up, his fists tight, an ugly distorted mask on his face as he surged toward Johnson. The street fighter felt no pressure. He simply kicked out with his boot slamming it into Hardy's face, smashing off three teeth, pulping his lips between teeth and boot, and hammering his nose so it bled again. Hardy fell to the side and rolled on the floor in agony.

"Sweet little cunt, Wendy," Johnson went on

as if nothing had happened. "Only way you gonna get junior hard down there is to use your mouth. You know how, suck it!"

She shook her head.

Johnson caught her hair with both hands and forced her face into his crotch, then pulled it back and flipped his penis up so she could take it.

"Eat it, slut, or I tell everyone about Girl, the little Sioux squaw and her bastard halfbreeds fucked up by your dear husband!"

Tears welled from her eyes. She shivered. Never had she felt so frightened, so alone, so in danger. This gone bad lawman could do anything he wanted, to the town, to her husband, to their business, to her . . . Slowly she opened her mouth and took his rod inside. She gagged, then made the adjustment and Johnson laughed.

"Damn, I think the little cunt has learned how to suck cock. Look at that! Best suck job I ever had. You're a most talented mouth, little bitch." He began to pump his hips back and forth, then slowed and stopped. "This isn't fun anymore."

He looked down at Hardy. The merchant had rolled around to see what was happening. His bloody, mashed-up face managed a furious glare.

Johnson lifted Wendy to her feet. She stood in front of him without moving, her eyes staring down but not at her husband.

"Yeah, now that's more like the proper respect. Let's see what's wrapped up in the package."

Before she could move he had caught the front of her dress in each hand and pulled sideways, popping the twenty buttons down the front from neck to navel. The dress tore apart showing her chemise.

"No!" she shrieked. "Stop that!" She tried to kick him, but missed. He laughed, pulled the dress down over her shoulders so it pinned her arms at her side. Then he took the thin, cotton chemise and ripped it off and let her breasts swing into view.

He had seen bigger, but these were here now.

Johnson felt the pain in his right shoulder where the bullet had gone in, but he was having too much fun to let it pain him that much. He grinned at her and bent and sucked on one of her breasts.

Just then Hardy swung his unloaded rifle by the barrel. He had aimed it at Johnson's head but when he bent to kiss her, it swooshed harmlessly over his back. Johnson saw it from his left eye, leaped back, grabbed the weapon, tore it from Hardy's hand and drove the butt hard into Hardy's stomach. The merchant doubled over and vomited on the floor, then curled up against the wall as spasms coursed through his aching body.

Johnson turned back to Wendy.

"Don't hurt him any more. He's my husband! Don't kill him. We'll do what you want!" She pushed the dress down off her arms, over her hips and stepped out of it, then unhooked the drawers and as he watched, she pushed them down a little at a time, teasing him.

Johnson stood there surprised, the rape aspect of his conquest was gone. She was giving it to him. Christ! He would still take it, make the old man watch him fucking his wife. Yeah!

"Just keep that cloth moving, sweet pussy," Johnson said. "You're going to get reamed out like the little guy there never did. You're gonna get yourself fucked by a real man." He bent and jerked the drawers off one of her legs, left them hanging on the other and grabbed her, sitting her on the top of the desk. He spread her legs and stepped between them, bent a little and nosed his shaft into her warm moist hole. He stopped.

"Hardy, you bastard. Stand up here and watch how a real man fucks your wife. Stand up, or so help me I'll blow your balls off with a .44 round!"

Dazed and unsure of what he was doing, Hardy stood and stared with unseeing eyes at the man in front of him. Then Johnson roared with laughter as he rammed hard into Wendy and heard her yelp in pain. She had to hold her arms around his neck to keep upright. Her legs trailed off the desk and he thundered into her body again and again, grunting like a bull, pulling her back to the front of the desk after he had pounded her away from him.

He lunged twice more into her, belched and pulled out of Wendy and pushed himself inside his pants.

"Now, little lady, you been fucked by the best, and don't you never forget it." He took a pair of deep breaths. "Back to business. Little lady, you listen to me good. If you don't want everybody in town to know about your husband's squaw and his two bastard breeds, you get that five thousand dollars for me by Tuesday. Then every week I come over here, you drop your drawers for me and give me five thousand. A simple, neat arrangement. You understand."

"Yes."

He turned to look at Hardy. She pulled the six-gun out of his holster and forgot to cock the trigger with her thumb. By the time she had pulled hard enough to cock the trigger so it would fire, Johnson had felt the gun move, and spun around, slamming the weapon just as it fired. The round roared downward, missed Johnson, and bored through Hardy's left leg.

"Fucking woman!" Johnson shouted as he backhanded her, hitting the side of her head and slamming her off the desk to the floor. He grabbed the gun and jammed it back in his holster, then stared at them both for a moment before he strode out the door and out of the building.

Jodi had stood frozen near the door to the office since she heard the first big argument. The shot had brought her back to life and she hurried into the room as soon as the sheriff stormed out. She found Mrs. Hardy rushing back into her clothes, and Mr. Hardy on the floor bleeding. She didn't say a word, she ran for Doc Paulson. He was in and just finishing with a patient. He rushed to the Emporium behind her and shook his head when he saw all the damage done to his friend.

"Looks like a locomotive ran over you, Hardy," he said. "Now don't talk. First let me get the bleeding stopped on that leg. Then we'll start patching you up—the worst parts first. Not a damn thing we can do about the teeth. Maybe someday we'll get a dentist in town. I don't even want to know who did all this to you."

"Sheriff Johnson did it," Wendy said. "He raped me and almost killed Hardy. When is somebody going to have enough courage to go up against him?" She paused a minute. "Maybe it's going to be up to me. Would you teach me to shoot a rifle, Doc?"

CHAPTER TWELVE

Spur moved like a shadow from the livery after paying for the dead horse. It was three blocks to the alley where the girls lived and he hoped the sheriff wasn't watching their door. It took him ten minutes to cover the distance, walking normally when he could, hiding in an alley mouth and behind a house as people went by. He wanted no one to see him knock on the door.

When he did, Rebecca opened it at once. She smiled at him and he saw she wore a print dress that buttoned high around her throat and had long sleeves and swept the floor. Good.

"You've been gone overnight," Rebecca said. "We missed you."

He looked quickly for that flash of anger in her eyes but saw none of it.

Spur touched her shoulder and she shivered. "Has Jodi said anything about the district attorney?"

"No."

It had been less than twenty-four hours. Spur left the rifle, got some more .44 rounds from his gear and smiled at Rebecca.

"I have to go out again, but I'll be back. You watch things for me." He touched her shoulder and checked the alley out the door. Clear. He closed the door after him and ran down the alley, crossed the street and walked casually along the far side of the street to the next alley and turned into it. This should be the alley in back of the Emporium. He hoped there was a sign on the back door.

It was almost noon when he slipped through the back door of the Emporium and looked around. A storage room. He went through it and checked a door on the far side. It opened into the main store. He saw Jodi behind the counter and whistled softly at her. She saw him and motioned him back, then came into the storage room.

Her face was strained, and he could tell she had been crying.

"Terrible! Just terrible. That damn sheriff came in here and had a fight with Hardy and mashed him up. He got shot in the leg and I think the sheriff raped Mrs. Hardy, and there was lots of screaming and yelling. I don't know what it was all about, but I do know the sheriff is demanding five thousand dollars a week from Hardy."

"Slow down, take it easy. Now tell me again what happened."

She did, as much as she knew.

"I sent them both home. I'm running the store the rest of the day. Lordy, I never seen a face so beat up as Hardy's was. Teeth broken off, ripped skin, smashed nose, just terrible."

"So, we have another nail in the sheriff's coffin. What about the district attorney. Do you know if he did anything about filing charges against the sheriff?"

Jodi frowned. "Strange. Clyde Oberholtzer was in the doctor's office when I went in with Hardy. Seems he had some cuts on his face and a loose tooth and a hurt side. He looked like he had been beat up too."

"Figures," Spur said. "So much for our big legal action charges to get rid of the sheriff."

"Oh, oh. Customer. Don't go away, I'll be right back." She went through the door and into the store.

When Jodi came back five minutes later she was white with shock. She showed Spur a flyer she carried. Spur read it:

WANTED DEAD OR ALIVE! REWARD $1,000. SPUR McCOY. LAST SEEN IN ELK CREEK, WYO. WANTED FOR ASSAULT ON SHERIFF'S DEPUTY AND THE MURDER OF A LAW ENFORCEMENT OFFICER. ARMED AND DANGEROUS.

There followed an accurate description of Spur. He read it, folded it neatly and put it in his shirt pocket.

"I'm making a collection of these. It's been tried before. It simply means I'm going to have to be more careful. So don't worry."

"But a thousand dollars! Spur, that's four year's wages for most men! There will be gunmen from all over looking for you."

"Probably, but I'll be watching for them. Why did Johnson get so violent with Hardy?"

"I don't know for sure. All I heard was something about the ranch he owns. I knew something terrible was going on in there but I didn't want to get caught up in it."

"Right, nobody can help anyone else when she's dead. Now, where does the district attorney live?"

She told him. "You be careful. With those wanted posters and all . . . Well, I want you at my place again, not splattered all over the street somewhere."

"You're terrific at descriptions," Spur said and laughed. "Don't worry, I'll watch my hindside. I don't want to wind up in boot hill out there either. I'll see you for supper, all right? I'm starved."

She held her face up to be kissed and he drew her tightly against him and kissed her three times, and left her gasping. Someone came in the front and she had to go out and clerk. Spur went to the back door, checked the alley, waited for a merchant to go back in his store. Spur headed down the alley heading toward the house where

130

the D.A. lived. It was a half block from the Hardy place.

Oberholtzer answered the knock on his back door himself. He had a bandage around his jaw, another on his forehead and he walked with deliberate caution. When he saw Spur he tried to close the door. Spur pushed it open slowly yet firmly.

"Sure it hurts to fight him," Spur said before Oberholtzer had a chance to say a word. "It's hurt me and this isn't even my town. Your job says you've got to expect a little hurt. At least you're still alive. Do you have a dead or alive wanted poster out on you?"

Oberholtzer shook his head.

Spur pulled the poster from his pocket. Oberholtzer shook his head in surprise. "I never thought he would go that far. The man is out of his mind."

"Now, tell me what happened with you and Johnson?"

"He came into the courthouse this morning and I served the papers on him. He laughed and tore them up. Then he punched me around until I fell down. When I was on the floor he began kicking me with his boots. If the two women hadn't come back from lunch right then I think he would have killed me."

"You're lucky, you have more charges to file against him. Assault and battery against a public official, attempted murder, conspiracy to murder. Write them up, and file them, but you don't have to give them to the sheriff. It's called piling up evidence. When we get enough I can take it to the

131

Territorial Governor and get some action from that level."

"If any of us are alive by then," Oberholtzer said. "I'm not going to work for a week. A vacation, I'm taking a vacation."

The man was scared. Spur had seen it before. There would be no more help from the district attorney. He cautioned Oberholtzer against going out of the house and faded out the back door.

Spur moved slowly, watching for tin stars on the chests of anyone on the street and worked his way to the back door of the newspaper office. It was unlocked. Spur stepped inside. He heard nothing, then someone began whistling near the front. Spur walked up and saw Les Van Dyke setting type at a type case. He had the eight point drawer out and was gathering body type for the next edition.

"I want three pages of advertising space every week for a year," Spur said.

Van Dyke jumped, surprised at the closeness of the voice, then he snorted.

"That's got to be McCoy. Nobody else in town has a wanted poster out on him, and nobody could be that cheerful when everything else around here is going to hell in a handbasket."

"You're still in business."

"Right, until this issue comes out. I've about decided to shoot it all in one big play and hope I can win."

"Don't do anything dumb, yet. We'll have our day, and it should be coming up fast. I think Johnson is getting worried. You know he beat up

132

Oberholtzer and then clobbered Hardy, making him look like a mummy."

"Hardy too? Why for god's sake?"

"Who knows? Something about blackmail. We've got enough to hang Johnson six times over if he wasn't the sheriff. We're so far off the beaten track up here, it would take us two weeks to get a company of militia up here. By then half the people in town would be dead. Looks like this is one we're going to have to take care of ourselves."

"We, meaning you," Van Dyke said. "The only thing I know about a .44 or a rifle is that they go bang. I'm a city boy. Don't count on me in your army. It sounds like you're talking about a civil war or at least a town-war shoot-out."

"I don't want it to come to that. Not good for the town, not good for all the people who wake up and find themselves dead. Hell of a shock."

"Speaking of dead, how do you plan on staying alive with a small fortune riding on your head?"

"First by staying here until it gets dark, then holing up in my favorite spot. I won't even tell you where it is."

"I don't want to know, in case I get tortured." He paused. "Can you set type, too?"

"A little rusty."

"Figures. Just some headlines with that twenty-four point. You should be able to find them. Here are half a dozen to start on."

Four hours later Spur cleaned the ink off his hands, then slipped into the darkness and made his way cautiously but quickly to the alley door.

The lock was open. He went inside then locked and bolted the door behind him.

Jodi stood at the stove working on dinner. Rebecca sat at the table. When she saw Spur she stood and smiled.

"Hope you like fried chicken," Jodi said. "That's what we're having. And some vegetables."

"Sounds fine. Hi, Rebecca."

She blushed, waved and then hurried into her room.

"I don't know what's got into her. She's been primping and looking in the mirror ever since I got home. Then she said it was my turn to cook dinner." Jodi turned, hands on her hips. "You haven't been romancing that girl, have you, Spur?"

"No. I did touch her hand and her shoulder the other day when she asked me to. She seems to be coming out of her shell a little."

"A little! Christ, Spur! This is the most progress she's made in five years. It's amazing. Whatever it is, just do it again. Maybe some day she'll be back to normal."

After they had supper Rebecca shooed them out of the kitchen since it was her turn to wash the dishes. The only place for them to go was Jodi's bedroom.

As soon as the door closed, Jodi kissed Spur hard. "I almost went crazy just now waiting until I could get you alone. Let me lock the door. There is not a chance that I'm going to let you get out of

134

here before you bounce me about three times on the bed, belly to belly!"

He caught her, picked her up and then dropped her on the bed. She giggled and began opening the top of her dress.

"No, no," Spur said, sitting beside her. "Don't do that, that is man's work. Besides, I enjoy tearing your clothes off that fantastic body."

"Good."

He opened the bodice of her dress and pushed his hand inside, finding one big breast and grabbing it. She smiled and kissed his lips.

"Faster, Spur, faster, I'm burning up."

He felt the heat coming from her whole body. It seared his hand on her breasts, pounded through her thighs to his, erupted from her crotch in a massive wave that warmed him through and through. He rolled on top of her and her hips began to pump upward against him.

"Sweetheart! Please, right now, please!"

He drew a pocket knife from his pants, opened a blade and knelt between her spread legs. Deftly he cut a slice through the crotch of her drawers. She yelped in sudden delight and jerked the buttons open on his fly.

A moment later she had pulled his hard penis out of its cloth jail and pushed it toward her heartland.

"Now, damnit, right now!"

Her hips were still gyrating. He nosed against her, her fingers helped position him and he slid into her slot, driving in hard and fast until his hips smashed against her pelvic bones and she moaned in total rapture and delight.

"Oh, god but that is good! I think I would have blown up if you hadn't come tonight. I was getting so horny I would have jumped the first bum to stagger down the alley. I just love you so much, Spur McCoy that I'm never going to let you go. You know that. Harder! Pound it into me harder! Each time you flick against my little clit down there and it sends me absolutely over the edge of the world!"

He slowed his pumping and then stopped, pushed a little lower and worked his face inside her partly opened dress and blew aside the chemise until he could pull one of her breasts into his mouth.

"Tits!" he said around his mouthful. "Best meal in the whole fucking world. Big tits, little tits, round ones, square ones, I don't care. I love tits! There, I said it!" He pushed his face between her breasts and flapped them back and forth hitting hard and chortling. "Beat to death by a pair of big tits."

"Shut up and fuck me," she said grinning.

"I am fucking you. What do you think this is? Making May Day baskets?"

"He's just laying there."

"Then you provide the action."

She tried humping against him, but he was too heavy for her to get much action. He growled and began again. She lifted her legs around his chest, then pushed them higher until they were at his arms. He nodded and moved so she could lift her legs on his shoulders. It lifted her hips higher and he drove in deeper still until she screeched in wonder.

"Christ, I've never tried this before!"

"I bet you will again."

"Oh, Jeez, oh jeez, oh jeez! OH JEEZ!!! I'M GOING TO EXPLODE!" Her face contorted, her whole body began to tremble and shake, jolting in one series of tremors after another. She cried out in the intense pain-pleasure of it a dozen times. Then she shattered in an earthquake spasm that left her sweating and moaning in ecstasy.

He felt his cock swelling inside her. As her spasm trailed off, his began. He drove hard so their pelvic bones grated and crashed, swept apart and ruptured into each other again.

His moaning matched hers in intensity, then he trailed off and shuddered one more time, driving his hips into her to plant his seed.

He let her legs slip over his arms to the bed. They lay that way for ten minutes before he pushed off her and lay by her side. Slowly, gently, they undressed each other. It took them ten minutes, a tender demonstration of feeling for each other.

"Now that was a good one," Jodi said reaching up and kissing his cheek. "Why is it always better with you, can you tell me that?"

"Anticipation always improves things," he said.

"Not this much, not a chance." She looked away, then leaned up on her side so she could see him better. She traced his chin with her finger. "You won't be around here long, I know that. You're no regular man, I understand that. You're here to get rid of our sheriff, one way or the other, and I just pray that it doesn't get you killed. But I know that after it's all over, you will be moving on, to somewhere else where there's trouble."

He leaned up and kissed her.

"No, let me finish. You probably have a girl in every town you stop in. I know I can't keep you here, and I'm damn sure that I can't go with you. So I want the rest of these days to be ones that you will remember all your life. I want to do anything, anything that you want to do. Just tell me, or show me. Anything!"

He kissed her. "Jodi, that was tender, and moving, and sincere, and I *will* remember it always." He kissed her again and she rolled against him, her hand reaching to his crotch, finding him and working slowly to bring him back to life.

Tenderly she brought him to his full erection, then moved Spur on his back, spread his legs and took him in her mouth.

"I want to make love to you every way I know how, and I want to do it all tonight. I'm glad we have an early start."

Then she worked on him, teased him until he could stand it no more and loosed his second load which she took and swallowed and licked him clean and then lay beside him as he rested.

138

"This is going to be the most remarkable and wonderful night that I've ever had," Jodi said. "I know damn well I'm going to remember it forever. And that's a gold-plated promise!"

CHAPTER THIRTEEN

Wendy Hardy waited until her husband fell asleep that evening. When she put the children to bed, she told them to be extremely quiet because their father was hurt and needed a long sleep. When they were quiet and sleeping, she checked the clock in the living room. Just after nine P.M. and dark outside.

She locked the house and walked quickly to the store, unlocked the back door and went to the Emporium gun case. She took out a Spencer repeater rifle. When they were first married, Hardy had taught her to shoot. He had upgraded her education every year or so, showing her the new rifles and pistols. She was good with guns. She loaded the tube with seven of the big .52 caliber rounds and slid it into place, then worked the lever on the bottom of the stock, loading a round in the chamber. It was ready to fire seven times.

The weapon was heavy, over ten pounds and was forty-seven inches long, but she could handle it. She went to the upstairs of the Emporium and worked her way to the front of the storage area. Some day they would make the whole upstairs into a retail area. She wanted all the women's things there, but that had to wait. None of the windows opened. She looked through one window and frowned. It was not right. She could not see the sheriff's office.

She knew his routine. Every night about ten the sheriff and his two deputies began checking doors and walking through the saloons. She wanted to greet Johnson the moment he walked out of the office, while he was still lighted by the lamp light from the windows.

But this wouldn't work. She went downstairs, put the rifle in a long cardboard box and went out the back door. She walked down the alley and into the alley behind the next block. This should work fine. The Hartford hotel was here and the unoccupied rooms would not be locked.

She went up the Hartford hotel's back stairway to the second floor when no one was watching, and found the room she wanted. It was open. She stepped inside, closed and locked the door, then pushed a chair under the door. She looked out the window.

Perfect! She could see the sheriff's office on the street that dead ended into the hotel and formed a "T." Quietly she lifted the window a foot and looked out. Yes. It would work. She sighed it over the sliding rear sight and the blade front sight nodded. Then she pulled another chair over, rested the barrel of the rifle on the window ledge and waited.

Once she dropped off to sleep, but she snapped awake quickly. She remembered what the beast, the non-human, had done to Hardy and she bristled with fury. She had not been shocked or angry with Johnson raping her. No, it hadn't been rape. It started out that way, but she allowed it, she even helped at that point. It meant nothing. Her body was certainly no holy temple that had been violated. One man's penis was the same as another's. The experience was distasteful but not earth shattering.

What she was furious about was the way Johnson had beaten her husband, had threatened her future and the safety and well being of her family, her children. She was a furious sow bear protecting her cubs, and no one, neither Sheriff Johnson nor anyone else, was going to threaten them.

Someone came out of the office and she tensed, but she could see it was not the sheriff. She would recognize his bulk and the high-crowned hat he wore. He insisted all of his deputies wear low-crowned hats with a badge pinned to the crown.

143

It was a type of uniform.

Then she admitted the other reason she wanted to kill the sheriff. He had confirmed what she had suspected for a long time, that Hardy had a mistress at the ranch. She had never been able to prove anything beyond her own intuition. He was always subtly different when he came back from the ranch. More tender, concerned. He thought more of her wants and needs for a day or two, almost as if in compensation. And now she could tell that it had been. He was making it up to her without her knowing it.

Dear sweet Hardy. The last man she would suspect of having another woman. It didn't bother her that the mistress was an Indian. She did not have the terror, the fear, the anger and hatred for the Indians most of the people in town did. They were people to her, like anyone else. Uneducated, with no advantages, but people nonetheless who had been pushed off their rightful property ever since the Pilgrims arrived in Jamestown in 1607.

She had not worked hard for fifteen years to have it all blown away in one morning! She would fight for her husband and her family in the only way that Tyler Johnson understood—force. She would return hurt for hurt! If only she could have remembered to cock the pistol with her thumb in the store that morning, the sheriff might be dead by now.

She firmed her resolve as someone else came out the door of the jail. It was Sheriff Johnson. She sighted down on him, his chest, the best target. She knew the first shot was most

144

important. She would have more time. After that she would be working the lever to push a new shell in and have to re-aim and he would be running for cover.

Wendy Hardy watched her target stop and look down the street. The blade sight centered on his chest and she squeezed the trigger the way Hardy taught her. The sound of the rifle going off deafened her in the small room. She saw the sheriff grab at his shoulder.

Damn!

Furiously she levered in a new round and aimed again where he had been. The sheriff had jumped behind a post holding up the front overhang of the jail. She fired again. The round slammed into the post. Four more times she aimed and fired. Her target surged back inside the door of the jail and she sent the last two rounds into the door, then dropped the weapon and looked into the hallway. No one. She stepped out and walked down the hall to the back stairs, went down them and into the alley just as she heard shouts at the front of the hotel and footsteps pounding up the front stairs.

Wendy Hardy walked through the alley, and back to her house. She had hit him, in the shoulder she guessed. The rifle must have been off in its aim. She should have "sighted it in" as Hardy had explained. Any rifle has a tendency to fire to one side or the other or slightly up or down. To make a weapon totally accurate, the sights can be adjusted, or the shooter simply takes the variance into account when she shoots.

145

Besides she wasn't a marksman. She had missed.

As she walked, Wendy evaluated her thoughts. She felt little different than she had when she had been planning the attack. She was still tremendously angry at the sheriff. She was angry at the system which permitted him to run rough-shod over them for so long. But she did not consider herself an outlaw or a criminal because she had deliberately tried to kill a man. He had it coming, she was totally justified. The only difference now was the sadness that she had missed, and that she probably wouldn't have another chance.

She had been home only five minutes when someone knocked on the front door.

When she opened the door she saw Deputy Sheriff Eliason. He was a crude character she had met in the store a few times.

"Mrs. Hardy?"

"Yes Mr. Eliason. What do you want? Hasn't your office caused me and my husband enough pain and suffering for one day?"

"Pardon, Ma'am. I was just supposed to find out if you was home. You been here all evening?"

"Of course. I'm not the kind of woman who goes parading around at night. Especially in Elk Creek where a decent woman isn't safe on the streets after dark. I want the sheriff to do some-thing about that!"

"Yes, Ma'am. I'll surely tell the sheriff."

He turned and went down the walk without another word. Wendy smiled as she closed the door. She had lied so easily! When you have a just cause lying was not that hard. So the sheriff had suspected her. It was a good thing she walked home quickly. He could never prove that she fired the weapon. And there were a number of Spencer repeating rifles in town. She was safe for the moment.

What she had to do was come up with some way to kill the sheriff. Wendy lifted her eyebrows in surprise. Here she was thinking about, and planning, how to kill someone. She shrugged. It was the maternal instinct. She was protecting her home and her family. That was power, a drive more powerful than anything the preacher ever said on Sunday morning.

Wendy went inside and checked on Hardy. He was sleeping soundly. For a moment she stared at his bandaged face. Poor dear! He would be months getting over the beating. And he had done it to protect her. She kissed the cheek that was not bandaged and he reached for her in his sleep. She caught his hands and put them by his side. Not yet, she thought, but soon. She had been forgetting to care for his needs. She knew that he needed to make love to her once a week. Maybe later tonight she would minister to him, start while he was sleeping and when he woke, she would tell him to lie still and she would do for him what he wanted. It was little enough for the pain he was in. In time she would learn to enjoy the feel of him in her mouth and even the taste. She put his hands down and went to look at her children.

All the while, Wendy Hardy was thinking of some way she could get another shot at the sheriff, how she could catch him unaware. She found the pistol Hardy kept in the drawer of his work bench. She loaded it, then unloaded it and practiced dry firing, thumbing back the hammer and sighting and firing quickly. When she was satisfied that she could do it accurately and quickly with both hands holding the heavy Remington, she loaded it, left an empty chamber under the hammer as Hardy had taught her, and slid the four-inch barrel .44 into her reticule. She would be ready now, if she had the chance.

CHAPTER FOURTEEN

The next morning Spur wrote a note, then edged into the alley and watched at the first side street until he saw a small boy running by. For a quarter the boy promised to deliver the note to the sheriff's office and forget what Spur looked like.

The note was to Deputy Sheriff Eliason, and said that he could earn fifty dollars quick and easy. He was not to tell the sheriff and to come to the corner of Main street and Wyoming Trail just as soon as he could. It would be easier if he came mounted.

Spur ran to the livery, rented a horse and

saddle, told the wrangler to forget he was there, and rode out of town and came back from the north approaching the meeting place just beyond a small creek and its green ribbon of narrow leafed cottonwood and trembling aspens. The Secret Service Agent stayed in the green cover until he made sure that the deputy rode out alone to the corner. There was only one house nearby, and Spur decided there had not been enough lead time for the deputy to plant a man there with a rifle.

Spur rode out with the Spencer rifle angled over the saddle at the deputy. When he saw Spur coming it was too late to draw.

"Just a little friendly protection," Spur said. He stared at Eliason, then nodded. "Wasn't sure if I recognized you or not, Eliason, but now I'm sure. We met in Dodge once and you were not a nice person at all."

"What the hell you talking about? I never been to Dodge." The deputy was nervous, his hands both on his saddle horn but his right itchy to draw.

"Got a poster in my gear that shows your face plain as day. It says dead or alive, friend. How you want it?"

"Ain't never been no wanteds out on me. Never! But I know who you are, and there is a wanted on you. A thousand dollars. That's worth my time to gun you down right here."

"You're forgetting the old Spencer here aimed right at your gut. I was disappointed in the reward they offered for you. Only three hundred.

Christ, you'd think a big man like you would be worth more than three hundred. It cost me half that to come to town and wait until I could identify you. But hell, every little bit counts."

"You ain't got me yet, McCoy, and what's more, you ain't got me hauled all the way back to Kansas. Don't spend your money too damn fast!"

"Just who the hell is there here to stop me? Your back shooting buddy turned up dead. You never were known as being fast with that six-gun even if you do tie it low, and me, I got seven .52 sweethearts in here just roaring to get out and punch holes in your three hundred dollar hide."

"Never make it. I told the sheriff I was coming out here."

"Shit! You lie worse than you rob banks, or whatever it was. Didn't say on the poster. You got a choice to make: you want to go to Kansas belly down across your saddle dead as a headless rattlesnake, or you want to ride head up? If you decide to go on breathing, you drop your iron over my side of that nag, and keep your hands back on the saddle horn . . ."

Eliason dove from his horse away from Spur. It was the move Spur expected and with the Spencer he fired by instinct. The round lanced through the vanishing shoulder, and Spur dug his heels into his mount, moving away from the area, and out of range of the Colt he knew the deputy had drawn.

Spur pulled up fifty yards away. He sent a rifle shot behind the sorrel which made the horse side step away from the deputy on the ground. One more shot moved the mount another ten yards and then she discovered some new grass at the edge of the trail and began feeding.

"No chance, Eliason. You got a slug in your shoulder, you want to try for one in your head?"

"Come get me."

"Not likely. I can sit out here and pick you to pieces, first your legs, then your arm. Maybe one round through your crotch just for fun. Sound interesting?"

There was a long silence. The deputy lay on the ground staring at Spur. The deputy had no cards in his hand to play with let alone a hand he could bluff.

"What do you really want, McCoy? You know damn well I'm not wanted anywhere. That don't work with me. I was going for you for the reward. That's four years pay for me."

"Not if you wind up dead. Make you a deal. You throw out the six-gun and I'll take you into town. We go in the back way and let the doctor dig out that slug, then I give you a sack of grub, your gun back and your horse. You ride like hell and I watch you out the first ten miles."

"What's to keep me from circling back and gunning you down for the reward?"

"Two things, Eliason. You sound like you could be a halfway honest lawman, if you had a chance. You're not too damn happy working for Johnson as it is. You know his charges against me and that damn reward are both a batch of lies. And if you come back and show your face in town, I'll blow your brains out."

There was another long silence, then Eliason stood, threw his six-gun on the ground. When it hit the ground it went off, the wild round zinging away from both men.

"Your play, McCoy. Somehow I was sure that Sheriff Johnson never would pay that reward money anyway. I get the feeling he's thinking about pulling up and getting out of town while he's still got his gold. He was telling me the other day he has over thirty thousand in the bank. I don't know whether to believe him or not."

Spur came up and searched the man quickly. He had a knife in his boot, but no other weapons.

On the ride to the doctor's office, Eliason told Spur about the attack on the sheriff the previous night.

"He took a rifle slug in the shoulder, but it went on through. He's furious. Doesn't know who shot him, but he's going to be accusing everyone. You're on top of his list. The doctor fixed him up, but he won't be charging around much for a day or two. Give me time to get well out of town."

"How many more deputies does the sheriff have?"

"Full time men was four, counting me. Now he's down to three, and one of them ain't too much count. You want to take over the office and jail, best time would be about six in the evening. Sheriff is at the hotel eating supper, and only one day deputy there. He's waiting to get off duty. Night men come on at seven. Be just two of them now and the sheriff."

"Thanks. I've got to take it sooner or later. Is

there a back door to the jail?"

"No, too hard to protect."

"Figures."

Doc Paulson lifted his brows when he saw another shoulder rifle wound, but said little. Spur talked with him as he waited for the bullet to come out. It had hit a bone and broken in half. Eliason's arm would have to be in a sling for a week.

"This is one gunshot wound I don't want you to report to the sheriff's office," Spur said. "Turned out to be an accident. You know how these things happen."

"Like happened to Hardy?"

"No, that was different. Going to cut down on those kind of accidents just as soon as possible. Eliason here is heading out of town for good."

"Happy trails," Doc said and stitched up the slice in Eliason's shoulder.

Spur spent another half hour getting a sack of food and supplies for Eliason from the Emporium. Then they rode out the back way. Eliason said he was heading for Sheridan. They rode east and when two hours had passed, Spur gave the man his six-gun and knife. He tossed him a box of shells.

"I want your word you'll keep on riding to Sheridan," Spur said. "I think you're a man of your word."

Eliason shrugged. "Hell, being on the move is better than waiting for somebody to gun down the whole sheriff's department back there in Elk Creek. Never have been too keen on getting myself shot. Hell, no! I won't be back. If I am it will be just as a traveler heading west." He tipped his hat, held the six-gun but didn't load it, and rode on east along the Greybull River and toward the Big Horn mountains.

Spur watched him for a few minutes, then rode back to town at a faster clip. He had business to get finished in Elk Creek before the sun went down.

The plan was *attrition.* Nick and scratch away at the sheriff's deputies until Johnson was alone, or nearly alone. Make him do his own dirty work and make him sweat and eventually flounder in his own blood. That was the plan.

Spur timed his ride back to town so he arrived at the livery stable ten minutes before six. He paid for his mount. Carrying the Spencer he moved slowly toward the sheriff's office and jail which were not in the courthouse with the other offices.

He paused in the alley across from the jail and waited. Sheriff Johnson came out and went up the street to the Hartford hotel for supper. Another deputy, Spur hadn't got a name for him yet, went the other way to a small eatery on the corner. Spur couldn't wait for darkness, sunset wouldn't come for at least two hours.

He walked out of the alley shadows, the Spencer in one hand in front of him, and strode casually to the jail, went a step past it, then returned and opened the door and stepped inside. When he closed the door he had his six-gun in hand and stared at Deputy Winslow who was eating his dinner.

"Hold it right there in mid-bite, Winslow, then come out from behind the counter and go flat on your face on the floor."

"What the hell? Hey, ain't you that wanted guy, McCoy?"

"Right and if you don't move in two seconds you're going to be dead!"

Winslow jumped up and did as he was told. Spur spotted some new manacles. They were steel wrist bands that snapped together and locked and held together with a chain six inches long. Spur used them on the deputy, cuffing his hands behind his back. Then Spur found what he was looking for, the stack of "wanted" posters on him. He made a small fire in metal trash basket and burned the sheets one at a time until they were all gone.

No one was in the jail cells. Spur prodded the deputy into the first cell and locked the door.

"Winslow, you look too bright to be hooked up with a loser like Johnson. Do you realize we have more than enough on him right now to hang him for murder? We do. And anybody on his team is going to come in for a whole bunch of hell. If we can prove that you pulled the trigger on any of those killings, you'll be wearing a necktie right beside Johnson on the gallows. Been a long time since this town has had a twin hanging. It will be an event!"

"Hey, I ain't never killed nobody. Pistol Pete was the executioner."

"Maybe so, but you knew about it. That makes

156

you an accomplice, and just as liable as Pete or the sheriff. You'll hang, no doubt about it."

"Unless what? What kind of a deal you got for me?"

"Deal? You trying to bribe me?"

"Shit yes! I know where the sheriff keeps a goodly sum of cash, his ride-out money he calls it. Must be six, maybe eight thousand dollars in there." Winslow was sounding worried, then scared.

"Look, they'll be back in a half hour. Let me out of here and let me ride out of town, and I'll show you that money. Is it a bargain?"

"How do I know you'll ride out?"

"Once that money is gone, the sheriff will suspect all us deputies. I better be gone or he'll kill me."

"You got a bargain," Spur said. He unlocked the jail cell, then the cuffs, and Winslow led Spur to the last of the four cells used for storage. He dug out a locked metal box at the bottom of the goods. He broke off the lock with a steel bar. Inside were sheafs of bank notes. Spur nodded and they headed for the front door.

As they did, Spur handed Winslow his six-gun. There were no rounds in it.

Winslow hesitated. "I ain't been paid for two months," he said.

Spur opened the metal box, took out five twenty dollar federal reserve notes and handed them to the ex-deputy. "That should hold you, now let's both get out of here."

At the door Spur saw a deputy. He pushed open

the door and came in, frowned at Spur as a flash of recognition came across his face.

Behind the deputy, Winslow raised his empty revolver and slammed the side of the heavy weapon down across the other man's skull. The struck man went down as if every muscle in his body had relaxed at the same time.

"Thanks," Spur said and the two men walked out of the jail, Spur carrying the metal box and his Spencer rifle. They both moved into the alley where Winslow got on his horse and headed for the Emporium for some traveling goods. Spur walked the other way and after some judicious waiting and stalling, found his chance and went through the door into the alley that opened on the girls' rooms.

Jodi and Rebecca were there. It seemed that they had put on fancy dresses and they looked good enough to eat for dessert.

He stopped at the door and whistled. "What a pair of beautiful ladies!" he said. "Now I know why I come back here so often." He went to Jodi and kissed her cheek, then turned to Rebecca and before she could move or speak he kissed her cheek. Walking across the room he put the metal box on the table. "Come see what I liberated from the jail," Spur said.

The girls followed him and when he opened the lid they both screeched in amazement.

"Is it real?" Jodi asked.

"It's real."

"Whose is it?" Rebecca asked.

"It should belong to all those people in town

158

Sheriff Johnson stole from. He's also got a bank account or two."

Jodi was stunned by the cash. "How much is there?"

They looked at it closer. Each bundle was tied with a string and each had a piece of paper with a total on it. The eight stacks of cash totaled seven thousand, three hundred and forty dollars.

"I never believed that much money existed!" Rebecca said, her eyes wide.

Spur put it back in the metal box and handed it to Rebecca. "Keep this for me. We'll turn it over to the county authorities when this little ruction is all over."

"Oh, I couldn't!"

"Of course you can. Just put it under your bed or in a corner someplace. Nobody is going to come in here looking for it. Now, what about some supper? I've got work to do tonight. Is this hotel dining room open or not?"

CHAPTER FIFTEEN

Two more deputies! Spur McCoy had to find them, the two remaining deputies and scare them out of town, chase them out of town or shoot them. The choices were coming down close to the vest now. None of the usual ploys had worked, so it was back to basics.

He would stay on the side streets with the hope that he could catch one of them making his rounds. The plan offered few prospects, but at this point it was all he had.

Dusk was falling and Spur worked out of the alley carefully the long way, and angled up the street. A clerk hurried by on his way home, loosening his string tie and taking off his hat as he began relaxing. A saddle maker set quietly at his bench cutting leather and trying it in place. He waved through the open door.

Spur came to the alley and stepped in beside a clapboard side of the building and paused. A few rigs went past on Main Street half a block ahead, but most of the mounted traffic was quiet. Two cowboys from a nearby ranch rode in. Neither wore guns. Most men didn't in town. Probably half the town people didn't own a gun and wouldn't know how to shoot it if they found one.

Two men walked down the dusty street toward the alley. Both wore guns. It was fast growing dark. The men didn't seem to be together. One walked faster than the other. He was twenty feet beyond Spur in the alley before the other approached the dark slot. Then both men whirled, guns out aimed at him from thirty feet.

"Don't move, McCoy or you're buzzard bait!" one called.

Spur never hesitated. With the first recognition of "don't move" he dove into the shadows of the alley, rolled and came up running hard through the gloom for the far end.

"Stop!" someone shouted frantically in front of him. Spur had drawn his .44 as he ran, and now sent three shots into the darkness ahead, aiming at the sound. As the roar of the shots faded he heard a piercing scream just ahead, and saw a man down on his back, both hands holding a bloody spot on his chest.

Spur ran past, out of the far end of the alley and angled out of town. He heard the men running behind him. It wasn't dark enough for him to lose them quickly. It was going to take some time. He sprinted past a house, cut through the side yard to the next block and down a street to a big cottonwood tree.

Silently he slid behind the cottonwood and waited. Both men pounded the ground after him, but when they came to this street with few houses and a dozen large trees, they stopped.

He could hear them whispering forty yards ahead of him. They decided on their strategy. One came straight down the street toward Spur and his tree. The other ran to the next block and Spur guessed he would also move in Spur's direction.

When Spur was sure the second man had run through to the next block, he watched the guy ahead of him. He had to be a bounty hunter. He moved from tree to tree, checking each one carefully.

Spur picked up a rock near the tree and waited. The hunter came slowly, watching all hiding places. When he was three feet from Spur's cottonwood, Spur threw the rock behind the man. He spun around and Spur stepped out silently and cocked his six-gun two feet from the man's head.

"You even flinch, cowboy, and you're a dead man!"

"Oh, shit!"

"Drop the iron, now!"

The gun hit the ground and Spur brought his

weapon down on the hunter's head. It made a soft thunking sound, and the gunman folded up on the ground. Spur dragged him behind the tree, used the hunter's kerchief to tie his hands behind his back, and his belt to cinch the man's ankles together. Then Spur left, heading back the way he had come, hoping the last of the three hunters had gone in the other direction.

He walked casually, heading toward Main Street, still looking for the deputies.

The shot came from behind him, digging up dirt at his feet. He whirled, saw the gunman out of range, but running forward. Spur turned and ran down a cross street heading back out of town. It was almost fully dark now, but Spur saw that a full moon was shining, and already was blunting the black effect of the darkness.

Spur was quickly past the corner, using a house to shield him from the gunman. He pounded hard down the block and turned to find only one house between him and the rolling high plateau. No cover. It was enough to put fear into the heart of an old infantryman. Spur found a small depression and rolled into it, clearing a spot where he could see through the waist high grass at the end of the street near the house. A soft wind blew toward him.

He relaxed. The hunter would have to come and find him. So he had the advantage. The hunter would make noise as he moved. Spur saw the flare of what he guessed was a match thirty yards away at the edge of the grass. The man was lighting a cigarette? Then Spur felt the grass. It was dry, dead already. A firetrap! Spur sent five shots from the six-gun at the tiny flame, but he knew he was too late. He reloaded and watched as the flame spread, then caught by the breeze it spewed toward him rapidly. It crackled and snapped in the silent, warm night air.

Spur stood and worked his way away from the fire, bending over as he ran straight into the prairie. Only after a half mile did he circle to the left and begin walking back into town. It was a fifty-fifty chance the hunter would move this way to wait for him. And if the moonlight wasn't any brighter, there was almost no chance that the hunter could spot Spur coming back in.

A half hour later Spur was in town without his hunting companion. He decided he was too recognizable. He took off his brown leather vest and his low-crowned, tan hat with the string of Mexican silver coins around it and put both behind a box in an alley near Main Street. He walked up to the thoroughfare bare-headed. It might buy him a little more freedom.

Spur walked the length of Main Street twice, searching for the men with tin stars on their hats. He saw neither one. The sheriff would be on light duty for a few days. So who was keeping the store? When Spur went past the jail the lamps were on, but he couldn't see anyone inside. He checked in two saloons, standing at the bat wings, looking in, but saw neither lawman.

Spur had about given up when he took one more trip up the main avenue. He was at the far end of the four block long string of businesses when someone shouted behind him. Spur ignored it. The second shout was closer.

"Spur McCoy! I don't want to back shoot you, so turn around slow." Spur didn't react. "You, bastard! You with the black shirt and no hat, Spur McCoy. Turn around!"

Instead Spur dove to his left, drew his six-gun with his right hand as he hit on his left side, rolled and came up with the weapon trained where he had heard the voice. A short man with a full beard stood there, his weapon in a double handed grip as he sighted in on his moving target.

Spur fired first. The round caught the man in the left thigh. Before Spur saw where the bullet hit he fired twice more, the rounds slamming into the man's chest. He jolted backward, the gun dropped from his hands as he screamed and grabbed at his chest.

Spur got up, still holding his gun and walked up to the man. He was bleeding bad, but the rounds had missed his heart. He would live for a while.

"Why?" Spur asked.

"Damn reward. I could use that thousand dollars."

"First you have to live to enjoy it," Spur said. He pointed his Remington at the nearest gawker. "You, run and bring Doc Paulson. This man can live if he gets treatment. Move it, you, now!" The man unfroze and rushed off toward Doctor Paulson's office.

Spur waved at a bystander. "You, get over here and hold his head out of the dirt. The man's hurt bad."

Spur faded into the thirty odd people who crowded around the man lying in the street, then walked away quickly into a side street. His hunting expedition had wound up with him turned into the rabbit instead of the hunter. It wasn't supposed to work that way. Jodi had been right. The bounty hunters were coming out of every street and alley in town. It would be worse tomorrow with daylight. By that time more men would have read about picking up a quick fortune for the cost of a .44 round.

Tomorrow he would send another note to the jail. Maybe he could coax one of the deputies out for a conference. No, he'd used that ploy and they would know what to expect. He needed some new plan. Maybe he could put something in the newspaper. But that would be too slow. Things were starting to come to a climax, Spur felt. However, he wasn't sure he had the right kind of control so that things would turn out the way he wanted.

Johnson was down and hurt, but not dead by a long shot. There had to be one final blow that would drive him out of office and out of town. But just what it was going to be, Spur didn't know. He had taken his best shots and come up short. If the two deputies stayed under cover, he had no chance to force them out of town. From five deputies down to two would hurt the sheriff, but he still had many built-in defenses. It was like a tough chess match.

How could Spur get in there and checkmate the sheriff? Spur thought of all the tricks in his magic bag, but had trouble finding one that would work.

The sheriff had been shot from ambush and would be doubly careful now. He was keeping his deputies on a close rein. He wasn't giving an inch on his legal right to enforce the laws of the land.

For just a moment Spur wished the bushwhacker could have nailed the sheriff through the heart. The trouble would be over and the town could get back to normal. He knew that wasn't the ideal way to solve a community law problem, but damn effective. The more he thought about it, the more he was resigned to the fact that eventually it would come down to a contest between himself and the sheriff. He could have done that the first day he hit town. No, he couldn't have. Spur McCoy was a lawman, not a hired assassin. He had to play it by the book of laws right up to the last possible moment. Then if nothing else worked, the standoff and showdown might be the only way, the last resort.

He was walking down a dark street when he heard footsteps behind him. He slowed and the other steps hurried forward. With a quickness that took the person behind him totally by surprise, Spur drew his weapon, whirled around and dropped to one knee, the big .44 aimed straight at the oncoming figure.

"Hold it!" Spur hissed.

"God, but you're good!" a thin teenage girl's voice said. "Don't worry, I won't hurt you, Spur McCoy. It's me, Violet, remember? I'm the little lady with the big tits."

He swore silently, put the weapon away and stood as she walked up to him. She took his arm and pulled it against her side, touching her breast as she urged him to walk forward.

"I've been looking for you. You've been busy, I know. Come in for a cup of coffee or some whiskey?"

"No."

She frowned up at him. "What's the matter? Scared? Afraid you can't handle all this woman?"

Spur chuckled. She was persistent. He stopped and caught both her shoulders.

"Miss Violet. I told you before, I don't get familiar with little girls. I don't like little girls, I like big girls. In two years you'll be a big girl."

"Aren't these big enough for you?" she said cupping her breasts through her blouse and lifting them.

"Plenty, it's upstairs in the brains department that isn't developed enough yet. Do you think it's all sex? Christ, you have a lot to learn."

"So start teaching me." She was rubbing his crotch with both her hands. He had to let go and step away.

"When you grow up a little more."

"Shit."

"Don't say that. Ladies don't talk that way."

"Goddamn."

"Don't swear."

"I could undress right here and scream and yell and accuse you of touching me, trying to rape me."

"True, you could do that. Which would put me in jail for five or ten years and you never would get to see me undressed."

"Christ, you and your logic. I know, don't swear. You can at least kiss me on the cheek as we say goodbye."

"Agreed." He bent to kiss her cheek, but she caught his head, turned it and she kissed him on the mouth, her tongue hard against his lips which he didn't open. At last he pulled away.

"Nice, huh?" she asked.

Spur grinned. "You little vixen. I should paddle you and send you home."

"Please paddle me!"

Spur laughed again, stepped back from her and walked quickly down the street before she tried something else. He wanted to see what Les Van Dyke was up to at the newspaper office. Maybe together they could work out some strategy to blast Sheriff Johnson right out of office!

CHAPTER SIXTEEN

The front door of the newspaper office was locked
but Spur McCoy saw lights in back, so he went
around to the alley and in through the unlocked
back door. Les Van Dyke was busy at the type
setting case and jumped a foot off his stool when
Spur said hello. He even reached for a six-gun
lying on top of the case.

"Christ, don't sneak up on me that way,
McCoy. I'm nervous enough as it is. Take a look
at the front of the place."

"Don't see why you're nervous. Nobody has
been shooting at you." Spur went through the

curtain to the front of the office. All the windows had been boarded up from the inside as well as the one big one from the outside. The door was barricaded with 2 x 4's which had been nailed across it. He saw two or three two-inch holes that had been bored in the boards. On the counter across the room lay two rifles, a shotgun and two pistols.

Spur went through the curtain and looked at the copy Van Dyke was setting.

"What the hell is going on? Looks like you're getting ready for a war."

"It will be, as soon as the paper hits the streets. If you'll help me we can have it out by early tomorrow morning."

"This isn't Wednesday night. Tomorrow isn't Thursday."

"So, this is a special edition. Already got the front page printed. Just two pages. Read it right over there."

Spur moved to the stack of printed sheets. He picked up the top one and looked at the two-inch high, double line of screaming headlines:

SHERIFF JOHNSON CHARGED WITH
GRAFT, MURDER, MALFEASANCE

The sub head covering three columns under it and leading into the news story said: *District Attorney Beaten Up When Papers Served on Johnson.*

Spur didn't need to read the rest. He shook his head and went over to Van Dyke.

"I thought you said you weren't going to do

172

anything stupid. This is stupid. This can get you killed."

"How? Johnson only has five deputies, no, four."

"Wrong, only two. Two of them decided to leave town today, with a little urging."

"Great, he'll probably only burn us out then."

"Us?"

"Sure, this is your operation. I'm just a newspaperman. If you shoot him it's all in the line of duty."

"You mean that arsenal up there is for me?"

"Told you, I'm a lousy shot."

"You set on doing this?"

"Right, I figure it's time. Better than ever if he only has two guns left. And him with a slug in his shoulder. I've got a story about him beating up on Hardy too. Not why, never really knew. But I cover Johnson's demand for $5,000 a week blackmail money."

"So you're lighting the fuse?"

"Damn right. That's why I wanted to deliver the copies in the morning. One will be on the porch of every house and business in town. There won't be a chance that the sheriff can pick up all the copies. Then if he comes after me, us, it will be in broad daylight for everyone to see."

"Just dandy. I'd one hell of a lot rather get shot in daylight than after dark."

"Hey, if he's just got two men, he might not even make a play. He might cut and run."

"Not without his mad money. One of the deputies showed me where he had stashed it."

"He's got his money in the bank."

"I'll have to see the banker tonight."

"What good will that do, Spur? Otto is a stickler for rules and procedures."

"Good—it will be easier for me to deal with him. I better see him before he goes to bed. Where does he live?"

Spur got directions and knocked on Otto Toller's door. The banker was small and round, with reddish fat cheeks and tufts of white hair. He was about sixty.

"Mr. Toller, my name is Spur McCoy. I need to talk to you about something if I could."

The banker beamed. "Heard you've been around town, and bothering our sheriff. Just who are you?"

Spur dug out his badge and showed it to the banker. "I'm with the United States Secret Service. As a banker you probably have heard of us. We worked for several years on nothing but counterfeiting, but now we deal with almost any crime local authorities can't handle."

"That answers a lot of my questions. What can I do for you?"

"I want you to put a federal freeze on any and all accounts that Tyler Johnson has access to. This includes all official and personal accounts."

"Usually it takes a federal judge to do that. Your badge helps, but I don't see how, legally, I could do that."

"Could you close tomorrow or the next day as an official bank holiday? Founders Day? That should do it."

"You're afraid that Tyler Johnson will plunder the county treasury and skip out of town?"

"I'd bet he will try within two days. The problem is the money he controls isn't his. He's been blackmailing and stealing it for years. You must know about all this."

The banker nodded. "Nobody could do anything about it. I've seen good friends of mine killed." He looked away, then back at Spur. "It didn't seem important enough to die over."

"Now it's different. The newspaper is going to come out with the facts, the bald truth. There could be a lot of trouble. You might want to close down the bank the day the paper comes out."

"Tomorrow?"

"I'm going to try to get Van Dyke to put it off one day."

"We always close down one day for accounting. When I see the paper come out with the story, I'll close the bank."

Spur shook his hand, put his badge away and went back to the newspaper.

"Why for God's sakes? I've just got up nerve enough to do it, now you want to hold off a day?" Les complained.

"A few things to clean up first. Things I want to get done before you blow the lid off this whole county. Might even save some lives if I can do what I want to."

"All right. One more day won't make that much difference. You get the bank to hold his cash?"

"Something like that. Now you won't need me

175

to help you print that other page."

"Coward."

"Work, my son, work. And don't forget to work out some way to barricade your back door."

Spur went out the back, watched others on the street, and got into the alley where the girls lived without attracting attention.

Jodi and Rebecca were sitting in rocking chairs sewing. Rebecca sat up and smiled.

"We heard there had been some shooting," she said. "Glad to see that you aren't dead."

Spur grinned. "Me too. The only dead I am is dead tired. I've got to get up early so I need to roll into bed early for a long sleep."

"Me too," Jodi said. "You understand, don't you, Rebecca?"

She nodded. "Yes. He's your man and you're going to make love. That's fine. I have more sewing to do." She looked at them and smiled.

Spur went into Jodi's bedroom and she followed.

"Amazing. My little sister is really developing. She's so much more grown up now, more realistic." She paused, frowned slightly, then put her arms around Spur. "We do have time for one or two quick ones, don't we?" She caught his hand and pushed it between their hips and between her legs.

Spur kissed her tenderly. "Jodi, for you I always have time for a quick one or two. Now get out of your clothes."

They made love softly, gently, and somehow she had a feeling this was how married love would be, more taking it for granted, not mountain top peaks every time. But a real, a solid love relationship, where both partners knew every move the other would make, and loved it.

She relaxed and let his hands caress her body, then returned the favor and soon they built and moved into delightful low key lovemaking.

"Hey, I could get used to this," Jodi said. She hurried on. "But I know, I shouldn't because you aren't going to be around that long and all the rest. So just let me dream a little, and love a lot, and hold you tightly while you are here so I have wonderful memories when my bed is empty and cold again."

Spur kissed her gently.

The next morning Rebecca slept in late. She had heard Jodi and Spur get up and smelled breakfast, but stayed in her room. Jodi knocked on Rebecca's door to say she was leaving and that Spur was already gone.

"Are you all right, Becky?"

"Yes, fine. Just sleepy."

"I'm going to work. You have an interesting day."

"Yes, I will."

Rebecca sat up in bed when she heard the outside door lock. She stretched, then lifted off the light cotton nightgown she wore and sat there nude. She usually didn't like to be naked. It was because *he* used to make her walk around the house for hours at a time all naked. *He* could touch her easier that way. She shivered. It had been months since she had felt strong enough to think about what *he* used to do. Now she felt good. She had been kissed by a man. She had not hurt him. Yes!

She got out of bed and stood in the room naked, then turned and looked at the small mirror over the dresser. It had been years since she had really looked at her body. Her breasts were round and pink tipped. Not as large as Jodi's but much larger than many women she used to see. Her glance left the mirror and she looked down at her body, breasts, thin waist, with a dark furry patch between her legs. She shivered again.

Rebecca dressed quickly, put on a modest dress that did not show her figure, went to the kitchen drawer a moment and then decided she would go for a walk. She could go to the edge of town and walk along the open country. Yes! It would feel good. When she was a girl she did a lot of walking. There might even be some wildflowers to pick!

Before she went out Rebecca looked in the mirror and decided a sunbonnet would be helpful. She found one that Jodi wore, put it on and went out the alley door.

Rebecca walked quickly through the alley, not because she was frightened, but because it was not pretty. She went down the street and hesitated which way to go when she came to Main Street. She decided to go north and was looking forward to finding some wildflowers in the prairie, when she bumped into a man on the boardwalk.

"Oh, sorry," she said stepping back.

Sheriff Tyler Johnson reached and caught her so she wouldn't fall. He stared down at her soft eyes and pretty face and smiled.

"Well, now. I might be shot up some, but I still know a pretty girl when I see one. I haven't seen much of you around town. What's your name?"

She tensed, then beat down the old furies and looked up.

"My name is Rebecca."

"Well, that's a nice name. Sorry I bumped into you. Sure you're not hurt?"

"No, I'm quite fine, thank you." She pulled away from him and it twinged the pain in his shoulder.

"You watch where you're walking now," the sheriff said, his glance following her as she walked down the street. He enjoyed the way her small bottom twitched the back of that dress.

Tyler Johnson was feeling better. The rifle slug in his shoulder was out and the pain easing. He needed some goddamn entertainment. Yeah, just some quick fun!

He had eaten a late breakfast, and belched softly as he followed her down the street in back of the blue and white calico dress. "Becky," he said softly. He had seen her around town, but not often. She was a real loner.

Fifteen minutes later Becky stood in the unspoiled prairie. It had been like this for thousands of years. She saw some yellowcups and bent to pick them. No more than two of anything because they were so beautiful growing there. She wanted others to be able to see them as well.

She saw some daisy blossoms ahead and ran to them. Before she realized it she had wandered a quarter of a mile from the last town street and found some wild roses. She was also down a small ravine and out of sight of town.

Sheriff Johnson had followed her patiently. When she slipped out of sight he grinned. He ran and found her sitting beside the start of a stream picking more wild flowers. He sat down beside her.

"Oh!" Rebecca said. "I didn't see you coming. Why are you here?"

"Why, to strip that dress off you and see your lucious, young, fucking body." He caught his hand in the bodice of her dress and pulled, but the stitches were strong and held. The sheriff swore and pulled her toward him, bending her into his lap. With both hands he jerked the cloth apart, tearing off buttons and exposing her chemise. He growled deep in his throat and tore the chemise away to expose her breasts.

"Yeah, nice," he said, and bent and kissed them.

Rebecca wanted to cry, but she couldn't. Anger shone out of her eyes. Then they took on a wild fury. She struggled to sit up, and he helped her.

"Oh, yes, sitting up that way makes your tits look bigger, don't it?"

Rebecca moved her hand slowly, felt in her skirts, but the pocket was trapped under her legs. She couldn't reach it!

He rubbed her breasts, grinned at her and

rubbed his crotch, then opened his fly and laughed. "You want to reel out my big cock, sweetheart?"

She shook her head. She had to move off her skirt to free the pocket. He moved enough so she could ease away from him and get up on her knees. His big hand caught one breast and held it tightly.

"Now, you ain't trying to get away are you, darling? You sit still and I'll show you big cock here and introduce you proper."

He got to his knees and unbuttoned his fly, then pulled out his hard penis. She couldn't look at it. Now she could get her right hand in her dress pocket.

"Want to bite on old cock here, Rebecca? He's good tasting, half the women in town can tell you that. Hell, take a bite."

Johnson caught her hair and the back of her neck and forced her head downward toward his crotch. She resisted, but he was stronger and his penis soon rubbed her cheeks, and across her mouth.

Rebecca wanted to vomit, but she gritted her teeth. She almost had her hand in her pocket. Then her fingers closed around the knife and she slid it from the pocket. Her hand with the long knife was behind her thigh now and he couldn't see it.

"What's the matter, Becky? You got to open your mouth to suck it. Come on, taste me. Ain't no big thing. My cock is the big thing!" He roared with laughter, and loosened his grip.

"Hell, after I get you a little warmed up I'll make you suck cock, whether you want to or not. Let's get the rest of that dress off. You want me to rip it off or will you take it off nice and easy?"

"I'll . . . I'll take it off."

"Yeah? Good. No tricks now. I'm stronger than you are, remember." He let loose of her neck and leaned back. She moved upward and turned slightly. He rubbed his penis a moment, then his hands came away from it.

She moved so quickly he never saw the swinging knife. The twelve-inch knife blade swung out from her hip and lifted upward two feet in front of Tyler Johnson's eyes before it reversed directions and in a hundredth of a second slashed downward with all Rebecca's strength.

Her aim was perfect. The heavy butcher knife blade hit in the center of his penis, and came with such force that it slashed through his genital member, chopping it off the way a heavy knife will slice a tree twig, with almost no movement of the still attached part.

The severed section dropped to the ground, and already Rebecca had thrown herself backward, away from the man. She scrambled to her feet and ran as fast as she could back toward town.

Behind her, Tyler Johnson slumped to the ground, sitting on his heels, his hand holding his severed stump. He grabbed his kerchief from around his throat and wrapped it as tightly as he could around his penis, holding it with his hand as he stood, and with shaky steps began plodding toward Doctor Paulson's office. If the sawbones said a word about this he would kill him!

He was dazed, shocked, so surprised he had not uttered a sound. As he walked the pain drilled through every nerve in his body. He screamed. He fell to his knees and held his decapitated member tenderly. Then he screeched out his fury for five minutes. He finally stood and, holding the blood soaked kerchief, ran as fast as he could to the back door of Doctor Paulson's office. Nobody was ever going to find out about this. And the girl, Rebecca, would die. She was as good as dead now. He would find out where she lived. In two or three days he would take care of her himself. But first he could cut her to pieces, cut her tits off, ream out her cunt with a red hot branding iron. Yes! He would treat her as violently as she did him. Then she would die.

Doctor Paulson heard the noise in back of his place and unlocked the door. He saw the sheriff, the blood soaked cloth at his crotch, and guessed what had happened.

Neither man said a word. The sheriff did not have to warn Doc Paulson. The medic quickly tied a tight cord around the shrunken, limp cut off penis. He heated up an iron and gave the sheriff a bottle of whiskey.

"Drink it all if you can, Sheriff. You're gonna need it." When the iron was hot the sheriff looked away. He gulped down another mouthful of the raw whiskey.

Doctor Paulson knew the bleeding had to be

stopped. The cord was not doing it. There was only one other way. The Romans used it three thousand years ago. The Egyptians had used it five thousand years ago.

He took the bottle from the sheriff, told him to stare at the wall, then brought the red-hot end of the soldering iron across the limp, bloody end of the penis. Tissues sizzled, blood vessels curled and seared shut, smoke lifted.

Sheriff Tyler screamed and swept Doctor Paulson and his infernal tool over the bench he lay on and dumped both on the floor. The pain was so outrageous, so totally debilitating, that Sheriff Tyler Johnson had time only to bellow his frustration, his pain, and his terror for five seconds before he fainted.

Doctor Paulson sat up on the floor and moved the still hot iron off his pants where it had burned a hole. He stared at the unconscious sheriff.

"Welcome back to the human race, Johnson," he said softly. "But I really don't think that you've got long to enjoy it. I just hope some small woman with a big knife did this to you. It's one hell of a lot better than castrating you. Now you'll still want to get a woman, but you damned well won't be able to!"

Doctor Paulson smiled thinly as he cleaned up the blood, put the iron away, then bandaged the shriveled penis and pushed it back in the sheriff's trousers. He even buttoned up the fly. Then he went back to his sick patients.

Three blocks away, Rebecca hurried down the alley and into her door. She locked it and then

184

went to the bedroom. She took off the torn dress, and put on another, then looked in the mirror.

I knew exactly what I was doing, she told the mirror. It was not a wild uncontrolled thing. I knew what the man was doing and I was defending myself. It wasn't at all like before. And it don't hurt. I don't hurt inside the way I used to when I used the knife. She smiled at the mirror and it smiled back at her. Yes, it was going to be all right.

Rebecca took the knife from the dress pocket and slowly, carefully ripped the pocket out of the skirt. She threw it away. Each day she would take another pocket from one of her skirts. She told herself the pockets were just to carry things, but she knew they were only for the knife.

Later she washed the butcher knife off carefully, scalded it to be sure it was clean, then put it back in the knife drawer.

Rebecca took the dress into the living room and sat in the rocking chair, patiently stitching up the damage, sewing on the ripped off buttons.

Yes, it was going to be just fine!

CHAPTER SEVENTEEN

Spur was up early that morning. He had breakfast with Jodi and hurried out of the alley just as it was getting light. He wanted to surprise the one deputy he figured would be on duty in the jail.

There was no one on the street as he came around the corner and walked in the dust of the street the half block down to the sheriff's office and jail. His boots would make no sound on the dirt but they would be heard on the boardwalk.

Spur went across the boards quietly to the jail door and tried the knob. Unlocked. He edged the door open slowly and peered inside. No one sat behind the desk. He eased inside the open door and stepped soundlessly across the board floor. The first jail cell was open. Two thin mattresses had been put on the bunk. A man Spur guessed was the deputy lay there sleeping soundly.

The Secret Service Agent moved inside the cell and lifted the six-gun from the man's holster that lay on the floor. He touched his shoulder.

Ira Lincoln came awake slowly, rubbed his eyes and sat up. Only then did he see Spur's six-gun aimed at his chest.

"Oh, damn, no!" Lincoln said.

"Afraid so. You a deputy sheriff?"

"I was. The sheriff said. What do you want?"

"Take a walk with me. I'll hold your six-gun. No, you can have it, soon as I take the stingers out of the cylinder." He removed the five rounds and pocketed them, then put the Colt in the deputy's holster. "Now, we take a walk."

They saw a rig driving into town, and two early risers moving toward an eatery. Otherwise no one was up yet in Elk Creek. Five minutes later they banged on the rear door of the newspaper office. It took another five minutes to wake up Les Van Dyke and get him to the door.

"You think this is a damned hotel or something, McCoy?" Van Dyke asked. Then he saw the other man. "That's one of Johnson's men."

"Was one of Johnson's men, mighty publisher of the truth. Now he's one of ours, or he's dead. Either way he wants to play it."

Lincoln looked up, curious. "What was all that?"

188

"You'll find out. You got those pages printed?"

"Yep, but no thanks to you."

"Good. We tie up Lincoln here and I'll help you spread the papers around town. We got Johnson down to one deputy, and Johnson himself beat up some. Don't think he'll get too nasty. What do you say?"

"Ink isn't dry yet. Didn't finish until almost five A.M. Then we got to fold them. Should be ready by noon if both of you help."

"We'll both be glad to help. Won't we, Lincoln?"

"Anything you say while you got the guns."

They were ready by noon. Spur tied Lincoln hand, foot and gagged him. Then they filled their arms with the two page paper. They split up, each beginning at opposite sides of town and working toward the center, putting a paper on every porch as well as in every store and shop.

As soon as Otto Toller saw the paper, he closed the bank and sent his two clerks home.

The deputy on duty at the sheriff's office closed and locked the front door and put out three loaded rifles, getting ready for any threat of mob action.

People began gathering in the street. Before three that afternoon more than half the four hundred people in town had gathered in front of the Emporium. Spur talked to them from the porch and called to get their attention.

"I hope you've read what Les Van Dyke had to say in the newspaper."

There were cheers and shouts and a gun shot or

two fired into the air.

"Most of the facts are there," Spur went on when he got them quieted down. "This county is going to have a legal sheriff's department, just as soon as we get rid of Johnson, and can hold an election. Is our district attorney here?"

There were some shouts in the crowd, and Clyde Oberholtzer came to the steps. He still wore two small bandages on his face, but his eyes were full of fire.

"Citizens of Elk Creek. We are about to root out his devil who grew in our midst. It was partly our own fault for not standing up to him before. I understand the sheriff has only one deputy left and he is barricaded in the jail. I don't know where the sheriff is, but let me warn you that this is no time for mob violence. We do not want a lynch mob here. If there is I will watch and arrest for murder every man who participates!

"We are through with law by force. We are going to have justice under the law, and that means a normal course of action. I have an arrest warrant for the sheriff, and I will serve it on him as soon as I can find him. If we have any specific charges against the two deputies still in town, they will be brought through normal legal channels.

"What I want now is for those of you with felony complaints against the sheriff or his deputies, to form a line over here and I'll listen to each of you. We need hard evidence, eye-witnesses to any crime. The more evidence we have, the better. Now line up over here and let me sharpen my pencil."

More than twenty people moved to one side, and the district attorney for River Bend County began taking down statements.

Spur got the crowd's attention again. "Does anyone know where the sheriff is right now?"

Doc Paulson spoke up. "He was in my office two hours ago for some minor surgery. My guess is he's in his rooms over the Golden Horseshoe saloon."

"Hold it!" Spur called. "Nobody is to go down there. That's my job. Now, do you have a mayor or a city council? I think they should say something, and they will need to talk to the county officials about getting a temporary sheriff appointed until an election can be held."

Someone stepped onto the porch. It was the saddle maker. He was the mayor of Elk Creek. As he talked Spur moved out of the crowd and toward the Golden Horseshoe. Two men with guns on their hips started to follow.

"Figured you might want some backup," one of them said.

"Can you use those hog legs?"

"Fair to middling," the other man said.

Spur waved them to follow him. He had picked up his Spencer earlier and twenty extra rounds. There were three rooms over the saloon. Access was up an outside stairway or through one built into the saloon. When Spur pushed open the door with the sheriff's name on it, he found a woman sitting on the bed, her dance call costume pulled down to the waist.

She looked up with tears streaming down her face. "He ain't here," she said. "He rode out almost an hour ago, right after he saw the paper. It's so awful, awful what they did to him. You should be ashamed of yourself, mutilating him that way!" She threw a pillow at Spur from the bed.

"Where was he heading, Miss?" Spur asked from just outside the door.

"I don't know. Wouldn't tell you if I did."

Spur and the two men went downstairs. There had been no horses tied outside the sheriff's office. That should mean they kept them at the livery.

Spur ran for the horse barns and found the wrangler.

"Did the sheriff ride out of here about an hour ago?"

"Yeah, he was still reading the paper. Did you read this thing?"

"Which way did he go?"

"Damned if I know. He was demanding five thousand dollars a month from old Hardy. Can you imagine that?"

"Yes. Get me a horse, a good one with some speed and lasting power. And a saddle. And rush it."

By the time Spur got mounted and rode away, he decided the sheriff would head for the biggest town. That would be Sheridan, two days' ride to the east. Cheyenne was ten days to the south and east.

McCoy rode east, found the trail and paused at a dusty spot to check the trail. A thin sprinkle the night before had settled the dust and wiped out previous wagon wheel and hoof prints in the dirt. Spur noticed the tracks of a heavily loaded horse galloping to the east. It was worth a try. He put the sorrel into a gentle canter and headed down the trail. The sheriff couldn't be more than an hour ahead of him. Sooner or later he would catch up.

By five that afternoon Spur hadn't caught him. A wagon loaded with freight from Sheridan came past and Spur asked the drivers about any riders ahead.

The redshirted teamster nodded. "Sure'n hell we seen somebody, but he sashayed off into the brush while we passed. Thought maybe he was a rawhider, but he looked too clean for that. Big guy on a dark gray dun."

"Thanks, neighbor."

Spur rode on. He pushed the horse now, riding at a hard gallop for a quarter mile, then letting her blow at a walk for a mile and hitting a six mile gait for a mile or so, then walking again.

McCoy came to a brush covered hill two miles farther on. The trail led straight down toward a river for five miles, without a turn or bend. He studied the trail dirt and saw the same hoof prints. Then far down a black blob moved forward. A horse and a rider.

The rider had to be Johnson. Spur did not want to spook the prey. He could get into the brush and hills and out of sight so Spur could never find him. As long as he stayed on the trail, he was a much better target. Far ahead Spur saw the trail swing to the right. It seemed to follow along the side of a ridge of hills and head toward a pass ten miles ahead. As Spur studied the landscape, he saw a thin trail of dust lift off a point where he thought the trail headed. It belonged to a wagon or a stagecoach. It was the main trail. Spur moved his horse into the trail, then cut to the right, following a stream. He would cut across the long arc to the left. He hoped to come out somewhere below the pass on the trail before Johnson got there.

Spur pushed the sorrel now. He made her work hard for an hour, figuring he was half way there. He put her into a gallop along an old trail that bordered the stream, and then cut across a small hill. A mile ahead he saw the slash of the trail through the trees. Again he pressed the sorrel and she responded. It would be dark in half an hour. He had to take Johnson before dusk or the sheriff could get away clean.

Twenty minutes later he was there. He tied the mare in a lush little glen of green grass and ran the last fifty yards to the trail. No single horse had been across here today. He checked for cover, picked out a big yellow pine near the trail to hide behind. The trembling aspen shaded the lower parts of the trail and kept Spur in the shadows.

He had a long drink from his canteen and waited for Tyler Johnson to come.

It was five minutes before he saw the dun plodding along up the trail. Johnson had his hat off, wiping his forehead. As he came closer Spur saw a curious thing. The sheriff sat on a pillow over the saddle. What was that all about?

Spur let him come forward. Spur brought up his Spencer seven shot repeating rifle, quietly chambered a round and waited.

There was little chance that Johnson would elect to go back to Elk Creek to stand trial. Prison would kill him. He would make a stand here. For a moment Spur wished he had picked a better spot for his ambush. The easy way would be to blow him out of the saddle without warning and straight into hell with a head shot from the Spencer. But that wasn't Spur McCoy's way. He had to give Johnson a chance to come in.

Spur sent the first shot from the Spencer just in front of the dun's head when the rider was thirty feet down the trail from Spur's big yellow pine.

Johnson did exactly what Spur would have done. He dove off the saddle away from the blue smoke of the shooter and rolled off the trail into a slight depression that half hid him. Spur had another shot but waited.

"There's no place to go, Johnson. I've got three men around you, one on your side of the trail almost in your hip pocket. Throw out your .44 and give it up. You'll get a fair trial back in Elk Creek."

"Fair trial?" Johnson roared. "You know damn well they'll hang me for everything that's happened in the county during the past three years."

"You deserve it, Johnson."

"Fuck you, McCoy. Come and get me." A six-gun blasted and the round hit the yellow pine.

"You're talking about one of us getting killed, Johnson. It sure as hell isn't going to be me. That just leaves you. You tired of the good life?"

"There isn't any good life on the end of a rope, McCoy, or in one of those frontier prisons." Another round smashed through leaves a foot over Spur's head. He ducked. When he looked again, Johnson was gone.

CHAPTER EIGHTEEN

Spur stared at the empty chunk of Wyoming wilderness. He had just spooked Johnson into the brush, it was only minutes away from darkness, and he didn't want to lose Johnson overnight. If so he might never find him again.

McCoy used the other man's horse as cover and darted across the narrow trail and dove into the woods. A pistol shot cracked ahead somewhere but the lead came nowhere near Spur. He stood behind a lodgepole pine almost big enough to hide him, and looked around it.

The faint blue haze of the .44 round's powder

charge smoke showed back down the trail. Johnson was hugging the trail so he wouldn't get lost, and would make a try for his horse again. Spur stood and keeping enough cover between him and the smoke, moved silently toward it. He stopped every six feet and listened. The third time he heard someone moving, then running ahead of him. Spur sprinted too, aiming at a large yellow pine ahead. He got there without getting shot, reached up on tip toes and looked around the tree.

Movement ahead.

It was there briefly and then gone. Spur resisted firing five shots at the spot hoping for a lucky hit. He tried to move when the sounds came ahead of him. Gradually he closed the distance between him and Johnson. The third time they moved and stopped he caught sight of Johnson sliding into some brush ahead, only twenty feet from the trail to their left.

There was no protection, no cover, for those twenty feet. Just a small clearing. Spur knew he couldn't wait. The sun was down, darkness would close in quickly. He pushed the six-gun ahead of him, blasted four shots as he charged across the opening. He had aimed into the spot he had seen Johnson disappear. Spur hoped for a lucky shot. He would take Johnson now anyway he could get him. Time was running out.

There was no answering rounds, but also no scream of pain. Missed. Spur had rolled behind a log near the far side of the clearing and now lifted himself over it. Ahead he saw another clearing past a dozen feet of brush. Johnson was running across it, but not really running, a kind of limp legged hopping motion.

Spur pulled up his Spencer and fired by instinct more than sighting and he saw Johnson go down as his left leg buckled under him and left him lying in the edge of the clearing. He dragged himself behind a log before Spur could get off another shot.

As quickly as possible, Spur pulled out the spent cartridges and pushed six new ones into his revolver. He had been moving through the brush, and now paused at the edge of the woods, still in the shadows and out of sight. There was more open space behind the log. Johnson was still there.

"Give it up, Johnson. I can patch you up, get you back to town."

A pistol cracked and heavy lead slanted through the brush near Spur. He darted behind a lodgepole pine and frowned.

"I won't execute you, Johnson. My job is to take you in alive. That's why I didn't heart shoot you. Talk to me."

"Go to hell."

"I've been there, it's no fun. Is that where you're heading?"

Another shot came from the ex-sheriff.

"That must be it!" Johnson said sounding more cheerful. "You're a goddamn bounty hunter. Hell, I'll pay you more than they will. How much do you want?"

"Eighty-five thousand dollars."

"Eighty-five . . . you're joking. I've got money in my saddlebags. Yours. All of it. Over five thousand in bills and gold, you can kill me and take it, but you're not the type. Too pure."

"I'm not a bounty hunter, Johnson. I'm a United States Government Secret Service Agent. I work for Washington, go anywhere in the west. We heard about you. You were out of control out here. Somebody had to do something."

"So what do you make working for Washington, eighty dollars a month and expenses? I can give you five thousand dollars! Cash. Right now. No questions asked. Just ride back and say I got away clean. You'll never hear from me again."

"I can't do that." Spur put a rifle bullet just over the top of the log, shredding half an inch of wood.

"If you don't want the money, what do you want, McCoy?"

"I want you to throw out your six-guns, both of them, and the rifle. Then to walk out in the open."

"Then what?"

"Then I tie you to your saddle and ride you back to Elk Creek where you will answer to charges brought against you in open court."

"That will never happen. We went through that."

"You can't win. I winged you in the leg, you had some kind of surgery, you've had two bullets in your shoulder within the last two days. You're about washed up, Johnson."

"Not while I breathe. In five minutes it'll be

dark, then I'll be away from you for good."

Spur left the pine and circled the small clearing. It was not more than twenty yards across, but it seemed forever for him to get around it. Another thirty feet and he would be able to see behind the log where Johnson lay. McCoy moved cautiously, then saw the log, and the first dullness of dusk settled over the woods.

Spur lifted the Spencer and called to Johnson.

"Don't move, Johnson, I've got your chest in my sights. Hold it! That's better. Now throw that revolver into the brush over the log."

Johnson did.

"Good, now the other one from your left holster."

"Gone, lost it on my run."

"Then stand up, slowly."

Johnson did. "Hit my arm with that first pistol round." The arm hung at his side. Too late Spur realized his mistake. Johnson's arm wasn't hurt, he had hidden the other six-gun behind his leg. The hand came up waist high and fired as Spur fired. The rifle slug drove into Johnson's chest, slashing through his left lung, spinning him backward, the .44 dropping from his hand.

Spur charged forward, his six-gun ready. Quickly he saw the man was badly wounded. He lay half over the log, blood pumped from his shirt and Spur saw the weapon out of reach. He knelt beside the ex-sheriff and used his kerchief to stop the blood. He wasn't sure if the round went out Johnson's back or not. The man's eyes blinked, and he tried to laugh, but couldn't. His breathing

201

came in ragged gasps.

"Breathe slow and easy," Spur said. "You're hit in the lung and it will be hard. You're hurt bad, but not dead. I can still get you into town. Did you bring any camping gear with you on that nag?"

"Yes, but you won't get me to town. End it right here. This hurts too damn bad to move, let alone ride back to town."

"You'll make it fine." Spur picked up the two pistols, searched Johnson and found a derringer in his boot and a knife. Spur took both, then lifted Johnson down so he was leaning against the log. The half sitting position made it easier on his breathing.

"Don't go away, I'll be right back."

Spur jogged through the mountain air to his horse, rode it back to Johnson's mount, and led it down the trail, then into the brush fifty feet to where Johnson lay. Darkness swept in for the night as he got down from the horse and tied both to brush.

A half hour later he had blankets over Johnson, a camp fire made and had heated up baked beans and made coffee. There were hard rolls and some apple butter.

"You eat well when you travel, Johnson."

He ate, grudgingly, but began to think about some kind of a defense.

"Hell, I might beat all the charges yet. Pistol Pete did it all. It was his idea. Did you know that he held me a virtual prisoner? He was the brains behind it all."

"Right, Johnson. Sounds good. Now get some sleep so we can get an early start in the morning."

The next morning they were up with the sun and shook the chill out of their bones in the high country as Spur packed up the gear, then helped Johnson on board. He insisted on the pillow, and sat tenderly on the saddle.

Spur tied his hands to the saddle horn, but left his legs free. He put a lead rope on the dun's reins and moved out on the trail.

"I figure we will be there just after noon," Spur said.

Johnson stared at him silently.

They spent the next half hour on the trail. Spur had not ridden it and was surprised when the open woods turned thicker and the trail hugged the side of the bluff. It wasn't a wide wagon road, but with a lot of courage a teamster could make it past the narrow spots.

Spur held the lead rope as they came to the first narrow place in the trail. The side of the cliff had been cut away by someone. The other side of the bluff fell away a hundred feet almost straight down. That had been the brownish slash Spur had seen from across the valley when he made the short cut.

Johnson hadn't said much on the way, now he began chattering.

"Yes, I've decided I'm going to like going back, fight all the charges, get a good lawyer from Cheyenne. Prove that Pistol Pete did it all. Did you gun down Pete?"

Spur looked back. "Yes, we had a small conflict but we settled it with .44's."

"Thought so," Johnson said. Then he rode up beside Spur dangerously close to the dropoff.

"Spur McCoy, you can't win every time. Changed my mind, I'm not going back with you. You want to come along with me, you just keep holding onto that lead rope!"

Tyler Johnson, ex-sheriff of River Bend County Wyoming, drove his heels into the flanks on the dun he rode and jerked the reins suddenly to the left. The horse bolted, charged to the left without knowing where it led, trusting the rider, only to find out too late she had no solid ground under her feet.

Spur stared in surprise as the horse headed four feet away to the dropoff, then slanted over it. He let go of the lead at once and saw Johnson's horse and Johnson charge over the side and then drop. By the time Spur had his horse stopped, dismounted and crawled out to the edge of the bluff, he saw only a red smeared pulp of a body on a rock a hundred feet below. The horse had gone farther. It lay against a large boulder that had fallen from the cliff years ago. The dun had broken its back and died instantly. There was no movement.

McCoy sat there a moment staring down. He could not possibly bring up the body. It would take ropes and pulleys and a dozen men.

He would send out a team from the district attorney's office to prove to the county that Johnson was dead. It might be easier this way after all. The search party could also bring back the five thousand dollars from the saddlebags, if Johnson was telling the truth.

Spur relaxed, got back on his horse and munched on what was left of the hard biscuits he had put in his saddlebags. He also had evened up the supplies and put two cans of beans and a tin of canned beef in his bags as well. At least he wouldn't starve before he got to Elk Creek.

As he rode he began checking off things he had to do. The biggest part of his mission was completed. Now the wrap-up and the details. Some of the details might be most interesting.

CHAPTER NINETEEN

Day two dawned clear and warm in Elk Creek. Nehemiah Hardy was up early. His headaches were gone, his cheek was healing and the bullet hole in his leg was coming along fine according to Doc Paulson. The rest of his injuries were healing but would take time. After the kids had gone to bed last night he and Wendy had made love three times. They hadn't done that in five years. Between the lovemaking he had told her everything about Girl, how he met her and how their relationship had just developed naturally. She said she understood.

He had promised then to break off any romantic and sexual contact with Girl. Wendy said she was glad, and he promised to take her to the ranch so she could meet Girl, and be there when he said goodbye to her.

Now they were in a rented buggy, a stock of provisions for the ranch as usual in the small boot behind them and they were driving to the ranch. He had made the trip a thousand times, but none with the light heart, the clean spirit, the sense of right and truth that he felt his morning.

"I'm glad we're going," Hardy said.

Wendy looked up at him and those fifteen years of loving and depending on him spilled over. She blinked rapidly and couldn't speak as she put her arms around him and hugged him tightly. He looked down at her. He bent and kissed the top of her head.

"I love you so much, Hardy!" She said when she could speak. "I . . . I wish we could stop over there under the trees and make love in the grass."

Hardy grinned and swung the buggy into the grove. They were a mile out of town and no one was on the trail. He tied the reins and kissed his wife. Then he put his hands on her breasts and she murmured deep in her throat. He opened her dress right there in the buggy and petted her breasts which were warm already, the nipples lifting in anticipation.

"Darling Hardy, I have two requests. I . . . I want to be on top."

He was surprised. "Yes, sure."

"And then the second time, I want to gobble

208

you up." She paused and he frowned. "I want to take you in my mouth!"

Hardy couldn't believe his ears. She had always shied away from any oral contact. He nodded, and kissed both her breasts.

"Of course, sweetheart. Anything you want."

Then they got out of the buggy, spread a blanket but she folded it, undressed him, they lay in the grass and held out her arms to him.

Two hours later they arrived at his ranch. It had grown since he first began it as a form of employment and income for Girl and her relatives. Now it was a fine working ranch, with over three thousand head of cattle, a drive to the rail head every spring, and a crew of ten cowboys and a resident manager. The manager, who had also taken a squaw bride, was hard working and honest.

Hardy drove the buggy past the main ranch house to the Indian quarters. They had been improved over the years and now included four frame houses, a bunk house and a tribal meeting hall. There were over twenty Indians living there. All worked the ranch in summer and fall and wintered over for the spring work. In the winters the braves hunted, made bows and arrows, and the smarter ones learned English and the ways of the round eyes.

The largest of the frame houses was a five room affair. It contained a big kitchen with a fireplace and a big wood range that had a built on copper tank and copper coils that went over the firebox to heat the water. The sturdy oven door was

Hardy's favorite seat in the kitchen. It was a fine place to get your back warm on a winter day.

Girl came running from the house, but when she saw Wendy she slowed to a stop. Her plain face showed no emotion, but Hardy knew she was surprised and shocked. She had learned to speak English over the years, and had taught her children to speak English as well, but now her second language failed her and she greeted Hardy in an old dialect of the Sioux.

He waved to her, got out and helped Wendy down from the buggy. She had worn a plain print dress, high necked and long sleeves, a fashion that swept the dust with the skirt. She held Hardy's hand so tightly that it was painful, but he knew she was hurting inside more than he could imagine.

"Wendy, this is Girl," he said, as the two women looked at each other. It was totally unfair. Girl had known about Wendy and his other family for fourteen years. Yet she hadn't been warned that she would meet Wendy today. Wendy had known about Girl and Hardy's other family for only two days, and she knew and dreaded meeting Girl.

Wendy gave the briefest of nods.

Girl looked at Hardy quickly, then her glance came back to her rival and she nodded just as briefly. Wendy gave a big sigh and leaned forward. She took two steps and put her arms around Girl and hugged her. Tears glistened in Wendy's eyes.

"Girl, I'm glad to meet you. I don't hate you. I

hope you don't hate me."

The small Indian woman looked up at the roundeyed squaw in wonder. She thought this meeting would never take place. She had feared and dreaded it for fourteen years. But as each year slipped past, she believed more firmly that she and Mrs. Hardy would not meet.

Girl felt a strange moisture in her eyes.

"Welcome to my lodge, to my home," Girl said. She stepped back, looked at Wendy once more, then reached out and took her hand and led her rival into the neat, clean house. It was nearly eleven o'clock and Girl quickly provided coffee for Wendy and herself and a shot glass of whiskey for Hardy. She spoke in her basic English as she prepared food. Any visitor of rank must be fed in an Indian lodge. It was a custom that always had to be followed.

The conversation was strained at first. There was no one else in the house. As was the custom, both the children and the others who lived there, whoever they might be, left the moment they saw the white man arrive. They returned only at his or Girl's request. Hardy had no thought of bringing his two half-breed children out. It would be cruel to Wendy. Girl would not call them. He felt sure that Wendy would allow that part of his relationship to remain clouded.

Hardy hobbled to the buggy on his wounded leg and brought in the supplies. By the time he got back, he found Girl and Wendy looking over her sewing basket.

"There are so many new things you need,"

Wendy said. "I'll see that you have two new pair of scissors, and some better knives, and all the new threads. We have some packets of needles that can be used for almost anything, from silk to tough buffalo hide. Yes, and I'll send some patterns too, and a dozen kinds of cloth."

They talked about other things, cooking and housekeeping, and Wendy kept adding to her list: more cooking pots, silverware, dishes, bowls, a new washtub and two of the new washboards that made getting clothes clean so much easier.

For the noon meal, Girl took a pot of boiled chicken off the fire, laying out bread and soft cheese and jam and coffee.

"No potatoes," she said and frowned. "Hardy always likes meat and potatoes."

Hardy looked embarrassed. Wendy glanced at him, then laughed, and after that it was as if the two women were sisters more than rivals.

When Girl brought out cold milk for the meal, Wendy stared at it in surprise.

"How do you keep it so cold, Girl?"

"Ice in pit," she said.

Hardy nodded. "It's an old Indian custom that I'm going to move into town this winter. We dig an ice pond near the river, a flat place three feet deep and fill it with water from the river. After it freezes in the winter we move in with crosscut saws and cut the ice into blocks two feet square and two or three feet thick, however deep it freezes. Then we put it in a ten or twelve foot deep hole we dug earlier before the ground froze. The pit is lined with hay or straw. We place straw between each layer of the ice, and then cover it up with a whole straw stack. I'm thinking of putting a roof over it to insulate it from the rain and sun.

"Inside it stays cold and frozen, and we have ice that way here at the ranch all the way into July on most years. We can do the same thing in town, and sell the ice during half the summer at a good price."

"What a wonderful idea! Every woman in town will thank you for that, Hardy."

They stayed for another two hours. Hardy was getting nervous. He went out for a tour of the ranch, talked with the manager for an hour and arranged for the sale of some stock to a young man who wanted to get started in the cattle business. They got on board the buggy. Girl had brought a two foot square of ice from the ice house and wrapped it in a blanket for the trip back to town.

Wendy stood near the smaller, dark Indian girl. She was barely thirty years old, four years younger than Wendy. She stepped forward and hugged the Indian girl again and smiled.

"I hope we can be friends. You know Hardy will not sleep with you anymore."

Girl nodded. "I know. Many years of happiness. Now I . . ." She stopped. They both knew she was about to say that she had her children to take care of and to love and to hope for. But she didn't say it. She touched Hardy on the shoulder, then turned and walked into the house.

There were tears in Wendy's eyes as she got into the buggy. She leaned against Hardy as they drove back toward town. When they came to the woods by the river where they had stopped that morning, she pointed to the spot and asked him to stop.

She got out of the buggy and led him to the grass beside the stream and drew his hands to her breasts. Without a word they made love again, gently, slowly and with more deep affection and appreciation than ever before.

She did not need to say anything to him, but he knew what she was thinking. Now he was truly her husband, and hers alone. Never again would he stray, never again would she worry about it, and they both could be good friends with Girl and her life at the ranch.

They got back in the buggy and hurried home now before the ice melted. They wanted to show it to the neighbors and the children.

CHAPTER TWENTY

Spur McCoy slipped into town quietly, put his horse into the livery and talked to Jodi a minute, then went on to see the mayor. The county commissioners were in session to pick a new temporary sheriff until one could be elected. Spur told the mayor that Johnson was dead and the new sheriff would have to go out and confirm it.

Then Spur went back to the girls' place to get his gear. He could take a room at the hotel now and not be shot in his sleep. When he knocked on the alley door, it came open almost at once, as if Rebecca had been waiting for him.

It was a little after ten o'clock. Spur was hungry. Rebecca fixed him breakfast and sat watching him eat it. When the things were cleared off the table and put away, she looked at Spur.

"Could we talk a minute before you move out?" she asked.

He nodded and they both sat on the couch.

"I guess Jodi told you about me," Rebecca said, her eyes wide, her face showing almost no emotion.

"We talked. She said you had an unhappy childhood."

"Yes, unhappy. My father molested me, sexually. He made me walk around the house without any clothes on. He did things to me that were strange and terrible. So one day I killed him."

"Yes, I know."

"For a long time I've hated all men."

"That's understandable."

"What Jodi doesn't know is that every once in a while I get so angry I go out at night and tease a man and then stab him. I killed some of them, I know." She showed him the pocket in her dress. "I tore out the pockets in all of my dresses except this one. I wanted to show it to you."

"But if you can talk about it, you are much better now. Did you know that?"

"Good! I hoped so. I owe it all to you. You helped me. You let me see a man as a person, not somebody always trying to push his . . . his thing, inside me."

216

"I'm glad I could help, Becky. You're a beautiful girl. I hope someday you get married."

"I might, but I'll need you to help me again. Did you find the sheriff?"

"Yes. He's dead."

Her brows lifted. "Good. I'm glad. He was a bad man. He tried to rape me yesterday. I felt so good I went for a walk to find some wildflowers. He followed me and ripped my dress down and felt me and opened his pants." She laughed. "Then I fooled him. I cut his pecker in half with my knife. But I didn't kill him. That's why I'm better. I don't need to kill a man anymore if he touches me."

Spur smiled. "Becky, you used your knife and cut part of the sheriff's penis off?"

"Yes, and he screamed and yelled and swore at me. I ran away."

"No wonder he was riding with a pillow on his saddle."

"Now, I want you to help me again." She reached over and kissed Spur on the lips. He kissed her back. She let her lips come away, and smiled.

"I like that. Once more?" She kissed him again and her lips opened and her tongue touched his lips then pulled back. She was like an eager teenager, curious, wondering. It was if she had forgotten the rapes, the molestations, as if that was in a different time, before her emotions had been fully developed.

She smiled and kissed him again, pushing herself against him, then easing back. The next time

217

she opened her lips his opened too. She let him dart his tongue into her mouth, and she nodded through the kiss.

She moved her hands as they kissed and he saw she was opening the buttons on her dress. He closed his hand over hers, stopping her.

"Rebecca, I don't want you to get excited and carried away. You don't have to do anything more. Why not let your future husband show you all about this?"

Her voice was small and soft. She shook her head as she blinked back tears. "No. I don't want to learn to love someone and have him love me, only to find that I can't let him love my body. I have to know for sure. Is that wrong?"

"No, Becky, not wrong at all. I think you deserve that much assurance. Are you sure you want me to help you?"

"Oh, yes! I'd love to marry you, but I know you like Jodi, and you bed her. I just want to find out for sure."

She moved his hand, then pushed it inside her dress and there was no other garment under it. His hand closed around her tender breast and he felt it throbbing.

Becky shuddered, then nodded. "Yes, darling, I like it. Yes, please go on."

She kissed him then, and she moaned softly. He touched her breast, then opened the dress top to her waist and pushed it back so both her breasts showed. They were beautiful, larger than he had guessed and tipped with dark red nipples centered on deep red aerolas.

"Yes, that feels good," she said.

He massaged them and caressed them, and at last reached down and kissed each breast, chewing a moment on the upraised nipples. She nodded.

"Yes, I remember now. Daddy used to suck on my tiny little titties. That's what he called them. Not so tiny now."

He felt her breathing faster, felt her move beside him. She turned and lay down on the couch. He followed her, lifted himself up so she could move her legs on the softness, then he lay on top of her, his growing hardness pressing against her soft belly and the void below at her crotch.

"Oh, yes, that feels nice."

He kissed her again, kissed her breasts, then put his hand on her leg and worked it up slowly. She gasped but she gritted her teeth and when he touched the softness between her legs, she smiled and nodded.

"Let me get out of them," Becky said. She pulled up her skirt and pushed down the drawers so she could kick them off her bare feet. When she lay down she kept her skirt bunched around her waist.

Spur kissed her breasts again, then knelt on the floor beside the couch and brought one hand up her inner thigh.

She shivered, then smiled again.

"Good, I haven't even tried to hurt you. It feels good. It's strange, as if I should stop you, as if I know it's going to hurt the way it used to when I was twelve when he pushed inside. Please, don't stop!"

His fingers brushed over her mound, then dove through the soft hair and touched the wetness and she jumped and screeched for just a moment.

"Oh, I remember now! It used to hurt like fire!"

"Maybe we should stop. You know it's going to be all right."

"No, he never could stop. I don't think that I could let you now. Please."

He opened his pants and worked his stiffness out. She looked at it and took a deep breath.

"Let me look."

He moved up so she could see his penis and scrotum. For a moment she experimented, played with him, then she nodded.

"I'm ready."

Spur lay beside her on the narrow cot. His hand found her heartland. His finger toyed with her a moment, then touched her clit and rubbed it six times. She climaxed, but it was over after one short surge of spasms. He touched her wet lips and rimmed them, then gently probed with one finger until he was deep inside her.

She blinked and looked at him, then she nodded. Spur sat up and went between her spread legs. He wet his throbbing penis with saliva and gently nudged toward her.

"No, no stop!" she said. Then she blinked back tears and shook her head. "You have to, I want you to. If you don't now I'll wither up and be an old maid all my life!"

He bent and kissed her tenderly. "You're sure?"

She nodded. "Yes, please, go ahead."

He touched his slippery tool to her wet lips and then pressed gently. There was some resistance, but not much, and he pressed in an inch, then slid past the guardian muscle which was still strong, and plunged deep inside her.

He could feel her relax.

"Oh, my! That is so easy, that feels so magnificent inside me. It's wonderful. It didn't hurt a bit!"

"It's not supposed to hurt. You're a grown woman now. A marvelously sexy, grown woman."

"Do I excite you?"

"As much as any woman I've ever made love to." He reached between them and found her love bud and twanged it again and again until she climaxed. This time she had relaxed and the tremors came one upon the other until she was moaning in pleasure. Her body shook as the climaxes built and built until she collapsed in a sweat.

"I've never . . . that was so . . . so . . . Oh, that was wonderful!"

Spur felt his own system peaking. He powered into her and felt her react. It was more benign then helpful as he thrust at her a dozen times before he shattered inside her and humped her into the couch until he was spent and drained. He fell on top of her, panting.

They lay quietly for five minutes. Then she squirmed and he moved away from her. She went and found a wet cloth and cleaned them both. They dressed and sat close to each other.

"Wonderful man, Spur McCoy. I know you came to town to get rid of our sheriff. But I am delighted that you found some time to help me while you were here. I'll always remember you. I'll never be the same again. I'm going to start going to church and going to socials and things. I won't be afraid to stay alone anymore. Maybe Jodi and I can find a little house somewhere in town so we won't have to live here in the alley. Then maybe I could help at the store. I know about housewares. If they do put in that new part, I'll talk to Jodi about it. Oh, I'll tell her what you did for me. She will understand. I didn't mean to come between you two. You still like her, don't you?"

"Yes, Becky. And I like you too."

"So we all can still be friends."

"We'll always be friends. Now, I think I better move into the hotel so anyone who wants to can find me. It's going to take a day or two more to get everything straightened out."

"I'll help you pack." She leaned in and kissed his cheek. "I'll always have you to thank for helping me. I'm not ready to get married tomorrow, but at least I know I will someday."

She helped him put everything in his carpet-bag.

"That knife case is for your kids," he said. "You can share the knives."

She looked at them for a minute, then nodded. "Yes, I can handle them now, too. A week ago, I couldn't have."

Spur pecked her on the lips at the door, said he would be back for a good dinner before he left, and walked quickly to the Hotel Hartford to register.

CHAPTER TWENTY-ONE

By noon Spur had registered in the hotel, talked to the mayor again and met a Mr. Ronkowski who said he was Chairman of the County Board of Supervisors. A new sheriff had been appointed to serve until the date of the next election, which had been set for two months away.

"Fred Denton is the new sheriff." Ronkowski said. "He doesn't know much about the law or being a lawman, but he's honest and a good church man. He'll do us fine for two months. He would like you to guide him to where Johnson jumped off the cliff."

"Be glad to. When?"

"He's ready to leave right now."

It turned out to be a little over ten miles to the death scene. They made it in two hours and Spur and the sheriff went down the cliff a half mile before they came to the dropoff. They could ride directly to the death scene this way. Tyler Johnson was little more than a mangled mass of bones and flesh. In the saddlebags still on the horse, they found the money. The sheriff carried it, and Spur tied Johnson's broken body on the pack horse they had brought along for the job. They rode back along the base of the cliff to the trail where the others met them and returned to town.

The job took a little over five hours, and the county came out nearly seven thousand dollars richer. Spur went back to Rebecca's rooms and took out the metal box of money.

"I had forgotten about it," Becky said. She touched Spur and smiled. "It's fun to be able to touch a man and not worry that I'm going to be hurt."

Spur fingered the cash. It was all there. He peeled off five hundred dollars and gave it to Becky. "I realize that an officer of the county assaulted, molested and attempted to rape you. If you'll accept this five hundred dollars, the county will deem the incident closed. That means you can't use the county to collect damages. Is that agreeable to you?"

Becky looked at the money and nodded. "Then we can buy a house in town somewhere!"

"Right, and have a lot left over."

Spur took the rest of the cash to the district attorney, who was working and trying to whistle past his bandages. Spur told him about finding the money in the jail, and that it must be county property. The district attorney smiled and made a record of the cash in the county books.

Over at the newspaper office, Spur saw Les Van Dyke taking the boards off all except the broken window. He was back in business.

"That deputy we had here," Van Dyke said. "I turned him over to the new sheriff who released him. Said there were no charges against him. Were some against the deputy who barricaded himself in the jail. He finally gave up and now is in a cell all his own."

Spur looked at the now famous newspaper that had triggered the outpouring of popular support. He grinned and pointed to the headlines.

"Did you know you spelled a word wrong in the headline?" Spur asked.

Van Dyke screeched. "Goddamnit, I didn't! Which one?"

Spur snorted. "You'll have to look it up. How are you going to learn to spell if somebody helps you all the time."

Spur left Van Dyke needlessly looking up each word in the headline, and headed for the sheriff office. Everything was under control.

The Secret Service Agent caught the banker just before he left for the night.

Otto Toller waved and waited.

"You need some banking business done, Mr. McCoy?"

"Not so you could notice. Just wondering how much cash our ex-sheriff had in his accounts?"

"District Attorney Oberholtzer was wondering that this morning. We checked every account with the Johnson name on it. He had four, and together there was just over twelve thousand dollars in them. We've put a hold on them and will use most of the money to repay any citizen who can substantiate a claim against the county because of the sheriff."

"Sounds like you'll run out of cash."

"We have set limits. We won't contest any claim for a thousand dollars for a misconduct death. Everything else is scaled down. Assault and battery as on the district attorney and Mr. Hardy would be medical expenses plus a hundred dollars. We're trying to be fair."

"Sounds reasonable. Well, looks like I've tied up all the loose ends. And I'm getting hungry. Mr. Toller, where is the best place in town to eat supper?"

The banker chuckled. "That's easy, Mr. McCoy. Best place in town is a cinch, no contest. It's at my table with Bessie cooking. Could I invite you to supper with us tonight?"

"Mr. Toller, your wife would kill you for bringing home company with no notice. I better try the hotel."

"No comparison. Besides, Mr. McCoy, I like your style, and the way you get things done. Now, it so happens I have a fine bank here, and my only kin is a pretty little daughter just old enough to get married. You care to come to supper to take a good look at her?"

Spur chuckled. "Mr. Toller, I'm honored. But I'm just not cut out to be a banker. Like to get out and move around. Plain hell on a woman. So I guess I must graciously refuse your kind invitation. Perhaps the next time I'm through town."

The banker closed his door, checked the locks, then waved at Spur and they went in opposite directions.

A few steps down the street someone grabbed his arm and held on. Spur looked down to see Jodi smiling up at him.

"Jodi, fancy meeting you here. Maybe you know where the best restaurant in town is?"

She nodded. "Trust me, I know. Did you get moved out?"

"Yes, to the Hartford."

"Good, that's where the best food in town is served, in your room. We order the steak for two and a whole baked pheasant, along with all the side dishes and it will cost you more than three dollars! It's a banquet. They've never served it before, but they will tonight. I get the idea your fiddle feet are itching again."

"Well, I am a working man."

She turned him into the Hartford, asked him to wait in the lobby while she gave the order at the dining room and came back a minute later.

"You're sure this is the best food in town?"

"That and a few nibbles on a certain delectable female, namely me."

"Now we are reaching full agreement."

A few minutes later, they lay side by side on the

bed in his room, both fully clothed as they talked. The food was due in half an hour.

"I had a long girl-to-girl conversation with Becky. She insists now that we call her Becky. She wants to get a job and that she is cured of whatever ailed her before. She also told me that you were there this afternoon and made love to her."

"True. It seemed like a good idea. A kind of therapy, a treatment. She has to learn that all men are not trying to hurt her. The whole thing was her idea. Do you think it helped?"

"Last time you kissed her and touched her breasts and she was practically cured. Now you fuck her once and she is an absolutely different person. I'd say you should go into being some kind of doctor for crazy people."

"You're not upset with me?"

"I am delighted with you. That's why tonight I am going to fuck your brains out."

Spur laughed. "Not until after we eat. I'm starved."

The food came complete with a fold-out special table and dishes steaming under two big covered trays. There was more food than Spur had seen in weeks, huge steaks, big baked potatoes, three vegetables, and the whole roasted pheasant on a platter with carving tools.

Spur saw Jodi open a bottle of wine and dug into the food as though he hadn't eaten in six days. He demolished the steak, tore off the pheasant drumstick and the breast and kept washing it down with wine. He had not enjoyed such a fine meal for years. He worked at stuffing himself until he could hardly move. They set the remains in the hall and locked the door.

Then both fell on the bed. Jodi kissed him.

"Not tonight, I have a stomache."

She laughed. "You should the way you ate, but I feel so sexy not I could go right on eating you."

She kissed him again.

"When are you leaving?"

"I missed the stage. Somebody said it went through yesterday. That means I ride to Sheridan tomorrow morning, or I wait here another week."

"Wait another week," she said unbuttoning his trousers.

"In another week I'd be worn down to a nub without the energy to lift my head."

"Which one?"

"Neither one."

"Shut up and make love to me."

"In my condition?"

"I'd rather have you seduce me," she said. "But in an emergency I can be terribly aggressive. Watch." She stripped his pants down, then took off his shirt. Soon he was naked.

"Your turn," he said. He lay there watching her strip and it brought a certain amount of desire. He sat up to watch better and soon she was sitting astride him lowering one breast after the other for him to kiss and chew on.

"Not bad, not bad," Jodi said. "Hey, you ever make love to sisters the same day before?"

"Not lately," he said and she pretended to hit him.

231

Things progressed rapidly. They made love and fell asleep in each other's arms. He woke up once and thought he heard something, then slept again.

When he woke up the next time, soft hands were playing with him. He turned in the dim light of the low lamp to tell Jodi to go back to sleep.

For a moment he stared in surprise. The naked girl beside him was not Jodi.

"Violet!" he whispered. "What are you doing here?"

"Just a friendly visit." She reached over and kissed him, pushing her bare breasts against his chest. When the kiss ended her hand had him hard and ready.

She pushed over on top of him and ground her hips against his hips and his stiff penis.

"I think you're ready, don't you?"

"Now wait a minute. Violet, I told you. You're too young."

"That's what you say." She lifted over him, aimed his lance at her hot sheath and lowered herself. "Really, do you think I'm that young?"

"You're not seventeen?"

"I used to say that. I'm nineteen."

Jodi laughed softly beside him. "True, this little cunt is nineteen and has been working the hotel for nearly two years. Some guys like to think they're poking a young girl."

"Jodi, I don't know where she came from, honest."

"Hey, I don't mind. I like to share things. Only you're mostly worn out. My turn isn't going to

232

come until after breakfast, I can tell you that."

"He's got plenty of action left," Violet said. "Just watch him."

Spur laced his fingers together and put them in back of his head. He lay there and listened, enjoying the two women arguing over him. It was going to be an interesting night, and most of tomorrow before he could get his gear together, hire a horse and ride to Sheridan.

Over him Violet began grinding with her hips and doing some strange things that brought him to life in a rush. Tomorrow, well, maybe he should lay over here for a day or two more and see if he could tire these two partners out. He should be able to outlast two little girls like these. If not, what a way to be beaten!